"I've decided to marry you," Lauren announced softly.

"Why, Lauren?" Cal asked, almost too quickly, then chided himself. She had accepted; why did he want to know why?

She turned back to cutting the vegetables for a garden salad, unable to look at Cal. "I'm doing it for Drew," she lied.

At that moment, Cal didn't care why she had decided to marry him again—all that mattered was that she had agreed to do it. He reached for her, turned her around to face him and cradled her gently in the circle of his embrace. She stiffened slightly before she melted against the solid hardness of his body.

Lauren curved her arms around Cal's waist, resting her cheek against his chest. It felt so good, so natural to be in his arms. She had not realized how much she missed his touch, his warmth. How much she had missed him.

Cal caught her chin between his thumb and forefinger. His gaze lingered longingly on her lovely face, focusing on her mouth. His head descended slowly and he staked his claim in a slow, drugging kiss.

Lauren rose on tiptoe, her arms going around his neck. She moaned softly as Cal devoured her mouth. An explosive heat swept through Lauren—a heat she had not felt in years.

The marriage wasn't for Drew. She had consented to remarry Caleb Samuels because she was still in love with him—she had never stopped loving him.

ROCHELLE ALERS

HAPPILY
EVER
AFTER

PINNACLE BOOKS
WINDSOR PUBLISHING CORP.

PINNACLE BOOKS are published by

Windsor Publishing Corp.
850 Third Ave
New York, NY 10022

The P logo Reg U.S. Pat & TM off. Pinnacle is a trademark
of Windsor Publishing Corp.

Second Pinnacle Printing: February, 1995

Printed in the United States of America

To Dr. Peter Conte—
for love, laughter and passion

Danelle Harmon—
for friendship and Historic Newburyport

and

Vivian Stephens—
for starting it all!

A man can inherit a house and money from his parents,
but only the Lord can give him a sensible wife.
Proverbs 19:14

Prologue

The taxi pulled away from the long line of yellow vehicles parked at the curbside arrivals at Logan Airport, heading for the Boston suburbs while the two passengers in the back seat were oblivious to the softly falling snow, the raucous honking of car and bus horns and the surreptitious glance the driver gave them in his rearview mirror.

Lauren Taylor-Samuels inched closer to her husband, luxuriating in his warmth and the now-familiar fragrance of his after-shave.

Cal Samuels smiled, threading the fingers of his right hand through the thick black hair falling around the shoulders of his wife.

His wife! The two words were the most reverent ones he had ever uttered in his life. A feeling of indescribable peace welled in his chest as he lowered his head and pressed his mouth to Lauren's soft, moist lips. She moaned under her breath and Cal deepened the kiss, easing her lips apart with his searching tongue.

Shifting slightly, his mouth traveled to an ear, over a closed eyelid and up to her flower-scented hair. "I can't get enough of you," he whispered for her ears only.

A light tinkling laugh filled the darkened interior of the taxi. "That's because you're insatiable," Lauren replied, her soft, husky voice fueling his rising passion.

Lauren's left hand was as busy as Cal's mouth when it slipped under his sweater, moving with agonizing slowness over his solid chest and down to his flat belly.

Her searching fingers elicited a tortured groan from Cal and he crushed Lauren to his side. He held her captive until the driver turned down the street to a home filled with heart-warming memories from his often unpredictable and sometimes turbulent childhood.

The taxi stopped in front of a three-story town house ablaze with golden light from the first and second floors. Lauren waited inside the taxi until the driver retrieved her luggage from the trunk and Cal paid him. Then anxiety, raw and uncontrollable shook her and there was no way she could hide her trembling from Cal as he grasped her hand to help her out of the car.

His free arm curved around her waist. "There's nothing to be nervous about. My grandfather will love you as much as I do."

She managed a small tight smile and followed Cal up the stairs. He inserted a key in the lock and the door opened into an entry filled with the muted glow from a Tiffany lamp, highlighting an antique drop-leaf table, two pull-up chairs, and the staircase leading to the upper levels.

He dropped her bags to the floor and captured both of her hands. "I'll introduce you to my grandfather, then I'll give you a tour of our apartment." *Our apartment.* Suddenly she was jolted into reality, her breath rushing from parted lips. "Are you all right, Lauren?" he asked, giving her a questioning look.

Lauren nodded numbly, unable to believe all that had happened and was happening to her. It was only now—after returning to Boston did she realize what she had done.

She had married a stranger—a man she had known for a week!

"Let me take your coat, darling." Lauren moved,

trancelike, as Cal helped her out of her coat and hung it in a closet with his. "Come with me," he urged, leading her through a spacious antique-filled living room. "Gramps is probably in his library."

Lauren missed the library's exquisite handwoven imported rug, the massive cherrywood furniture, the books packed tightly on floor-to-ceiling shelves and the framed artwork hanging on two facing walls, when the leonine head of the man seated on a blood-red brocade armchair came up slowly.

He rose to his feet and Lauren unconsciously took a backwards step. Cal's chest pressed against her back, not allowing her to move or escape.

"Gramps, this is Lauren—my wife. Lauren, my grandfather, Dr. Caleb Samuels."

Caleb Samuels's spare frame made him appear taller and more imposing than his six-foot height. A shock of pure white curling hair framed his angular dark-brown face, while his dark eyes glowing from that face rooted Lauren to the spot. He smiled a tight cold smile, inclining his head slightly.

Cal gave her a slight push and she was galvanized into action, remembering her manners. "I'm . . . I'm honored . . . Dr. Samuels."

The elder Caleb's smile widened, but it still lacked warmth. "You may address me as Gramps," he stated, making it sound as if Gramps was a royal title he had inherited from his father.

"Have you and Lauren eaten?" Dr. Samuels asked his grandson.

"We had a snack on the plane," Cal said, escorting Lauren to a love seat. He sat, pulling her down beside him.

"I'll have Mrs. Austin prepare a special dinner to celebrate your . . ." His voice trailed off as he returned to the armchair and stared at Lauren. "Your hasty marriage," he continued, redirecting his attention to Cal.

Lauren half-listened to the conversation between her new husband and his grandfather as she contemplated how she had taken leave of her senses.

Here she was sitting in the library of a world renowned geneticist and winner of a Nobel Prize for Medicine while he glared at her. There was no mistaking his disapproval.

Her throat grew dry as she realized Cal was wrong— his grandfather did not like her. Not liking her meant he would never love her.

She stared at the heavy gold signet ring which had adorned Cal's little finger and now graced her ring finger. The ring and the man sitting beside her were reminders of a week of madness. A madness in which she fell in love with, and married a stranger.

But did she love Cal? Did she love him enough to share her life with him? What had she done? The questions attacked her relentlessly as the realization of her impulsiveness clouded her face with uneasiness.

"Are you going to keep your maiden name, Lauren?" Dr. Samuels's question startled her. "I think I'll use Taylor professionally," she replied. "It would probably be a little confusing for Summit Publishing to have two Samuelses on their payroll." This disclosure seemed to please the elder Samuels because he gave Lauren his first sincere smile.

Cal's hand curved around her neck, bringing her head to his hard shoulder. "I think Mrs. Lauren Taylor-Samuels should rest before dinner. She's been up before dawn."

Dr. Samuels rose again. "Please forgive me. We'll talk later over dinner. Cal, put your bride to bed while I let Mrs. Austin know that we'll have company for dinner."

Perhaps it was her own uneasiness but Lauren recoiled when she registered Dr. Samuels's reference to her being company. She was his grandson's wife and therefore family, not company.

Cal needed no further prompting as he led Lauren up

a flight of stairs to the second floor. "Mrs. Austin has been Gramps' cook and housekeeper ever since my grandmother passed away fifteen years ago," he explained quietly. "They can't agree on anything, but Gramps won't fire her because he says he won't give her that satisfaction. He claims he's waiting for her to quit."

If Cal sought to lighten Lauren's mood, he failed. She stood in the middle of a large bedroom, staring up at him. "Your grandfather frightens me," she blurted out.

Cal wound his arms around her waist, pulling her close to his body. "I admit he's a little imposing when you first meet him but he's actually a pussycat, darling."

Cal's assessment of his grandfather did nothing to lessen Lauren's insecurity and she realized it wasn't the older man's disturbing presence as much as it was her own doubts and fear.

On Cay Verde it was all right for a twenty-two-year-old researcher to fall in love with best-selling writer C. B. Samuels and marry him after a week of passionate, unbridled lovemaking; but it seemed as if her sanity returned the moment she and Cal returned to a cold and snowy Boston, Massachusetts. The frigid wind cooled her passion, sweeping away the warm memories of the Caribbean island where she had lost herself in the lushness of the tropics and Caleb Samuels's expert seduction.

"Why don't you try to get some sleep," Cal suggested. He kissed the tip of her nose. "I don't want you to look as if I've kept you up all night when I get to meet your parents tomorrow."

Her parents. How was she to explain to her parents that she had married a stranger? She, Lauren Taylor, who had never done anything impulsive in her life had suddenly lost her heart and head to a sybaritic writer.

Lauren willed her mind to go blank before she dissolved into a paroxysm of tears. She undressed slowly and slipped into a nightgown after Cal returned with her luggage. She watched him watch her as she sat down on the edge of the bed she was to share with him. Could she pretend she loved him because at that moment she wasn't sure whether she truly did.

"Everything's going to be all right, darling," he said softly, as if reading her mind.

I hope you're right, she thought. Minutes later she lay in bed with Cal, staring up at the darkness. She ignored the hardness of his naked body pressing intimately to hers, feigning sleep. It was only when she heard his soft snores that she relaxed enough to find her own solace in sleep.

Lauren managed to finish her dinner without bolting from the table whenever she glanced up to find Dr. Caleb Samuels visually examining her. A shudder passed through her and somewhere she found the strength not to cry.

He hates me and I hate him.

How was she to live in a house with a man who hated her as much as he loved his grandson?

But he can't hate you, a little voice whispered in her head. He doesn't know you.

She drank two glasses of the rich red wine and it was enough to dull the misery pressing down on Lauren like a steel weight. She had made a mistake. She never should've married Cal. She didn't love him. She couldn't love him. She was too inexperienced to be a wife—especially to a man like Caleb Samuels.

Dr. Samuels touched a white linen napkin to his mouth. "I must excuse myself because I have a speaking engagement early tomorrow morning and I have to go over my notes before I turn in."

Leaning back in his chair, Cal nodded, smiling. "Good night, Gramps."

Lauren offered a small smile, mumbling, "Good night."

Cal waited until Dr. Samuels left the dining room, then reached across the table and refilled Lauren's glass. His golden-brown eyes lovingly caressed her delicate face. "I can't believe how lucky I am to have found you, Lauren." She rewarded him with a sensual smile.

Cal continued to stare at her as she sipped her wine. Could he see her fear, doubts? Did he know what she was thinking, feeling? He drained his glass, then rose to his feet and extended his hand across the table. "Let's go to bed."

Lauren did not protest when Cal gathered her in his arms and carried her up the staircase to their bedroom. She forgot about Dr. Samuels's censuring glares when she succumbed to the drugging effects of the wine, leaving Cal tossing restlessly until sleep overtook him.

Lauren lay staring up at the ceiling and waiting for dawn. She had reached a decision. What she was feeling now she felt when she first met him. She wanted away from him—out of his presence.

As Lauren Taylor the researcher she had held her own with him, but as Lauren Taylor the woman he had overwhelmed her, and she knew she had to put as much distance between herself and Caleb Samuels or she would never survive his dynamic personality. She wasn't equipped to continue the farce she had helped create.

He had called her a child when she was introduced to him, and how right he was. She thought she was a full-grown woman, but her impulsiveness had proven the contrary.

Cal registered her change in breathing and turned over to find Lauren wide awake. His hand began a leisurely exploration of her exposed thighs.

"Don't!" Lauren commanded, her hand stopping his.

Moving quickly, Cal straddled her body, supporting his weight on his arms. "What's the matter, darling?"

Lauren pushed against his shoulders. "I don't want you to touch me."

A frown creased his forehead. "Don't touch you or don't make love to you?"

"Both." He released her and Lauren sat up, pressing her back against the headboard.

Cal inhaled deeply, closing his eyes. "What's up, Lauren?"

She combed her mussed hair away from her forehead with her fingers. "I can't be married to you," she blurted out.

He smiled. "That's too late because we are married."

"What I mean is that I can't *remain* married to you." Lauren closed her eyes, not seeing the blood darken Cal's tanned face as his eyes flamed with liquid gold fire.

"Say it, Lauren." His voice had a tone of lethal softness that frightened her more than if he had shouted at her.

"I'm leaving you," Lauren said without hesitating.

"Why?"

"Because . . . because I don't love you. I made a mistake to agree to marry you." She reopened her eyes, registering his stoic expression, and at that moment he was a replica of his grandfather.

"I don't think I want to be married—not to you—not to anyone," she continued.

Cal stared at her, not moving or saying anything. If he had said something it would have made it easy—a lot easier for her.

Lauren panicked, tears filling her eyes and overflowing down her sable-brown cheeks. "Think of my happiness, Caleb!" she screamed.

Cal's gaze was cold, vacant and then he nodded. He hadn't said she could go, he just nodded.

Lauren never remembered dressing or packing her clothes or the taxi ride that took her home to her parents. She did remember walking into her mother's outstretched arms and collapsing with the pain and shame that shattered her into so many pieces that she wasn't certain whether she would ever be whole again.

* * *

Dr. Samuels returned in time to overhear the last of Cal's conversation before he replaced the telephone receiver on its cradle.

"Where are you going?"

Turning slowly, Cal stared at his grandfather. "Back to Spain?"

"Where is she?"

Cal's jaw hardened as he slipped his hands into the pockets of his slacks. "She's gone."

"And you let her go?"

"Yes, Gramps. I let her go."

"Why?"

In spite of his pain Cal managed a brittle smile. "I want her happy. I love her just that much."

"And she wasn't happy with you?"

"No." His mouth thinned to a hard thin line before he turned on his heel and stalked out of the library.

Dr. Samuels's gaunt frame swayed slightly before he moved over to his desk. It had begun again. It was like it was nearly thirty years ago, and it was happening again with another generation. He was not able to change the past, but he was damned if he wouldn't do something this time.

Picking up the telephone, he dialed a number. "I need you to do some research for me," he said without preamble. "I want you to check out a Lauren Taylor. She lives in Boston and works as a researcher for Summit Publishing." The person on the other end of the telephone line needed no additional information. Her name was enough.

Dr. Samuels replaced the receiver and smiled. His dark eyes danced with sinister triumph, because he would make certain Lauren Taylor-Samuels would pay for her deceit.

Chapter One

"When are you going to let Drew spend some time with me? You've lived here for nearly two months and in all of that time I've seen my grandson once. I can forgive you for everything else, but not that, Lauren Vernice Taylor."

Lauren peered calmly at her mother over the rim of a tall glass of iced tea. It was a familiar tirade. Even when she and Drew lived less than a mile from her parents, it was the same. Odessa Taylor complained bitterly that she did not see enough of her only grandchild.

"Drew has made new friends, Mama," Lauren replied in a quiet tone. "There're times when he doesn't want to come home to eat."

Odessa's delicate eyebrows formed an agonized frown. "You're not letting him eat with strangers, are you? Now, you know how I raised you, Lauren. Eat at your own table and sleep in your own bed."

Lauren gave Odessa a look that infuriated the older woman. "I can afford to feed my son and keep a roof over his head."

Deep color darkened Odessa's burnished-gold face and a sprinkling of freckles stood out in startling contrast across her nose and cheeks. At fifty-one she had given up trying to conceal them with makeup. Her clear brown eyes widened at Lauren's veiled retort.

"I know you can take care of your son, Lauren. You've proven that over the past four years."

Lauren placed her glass of tea on a table and moved closer to Odessa on the wicker love seat. Looping her arms around her neck, she pressed her lips to Odessa's stylishly coiffed short hair. "I'm sorry, Mama. I didn't mean to snap at you."

Odessa cradled Lauren to her shoulder. "Forgive me, baby. There are times when I can't stop being a mother."

Lauren's velvet black eyes caressed Odessa's exquisitely sculptured face. "No more than I can help being just like you, Mama. We may not look anything alike, but that doesn't change a thing. I *am* your daughter when I reprimand Drew that he doesn't need to sleep over at his friend's house because he has his own bed to sleep in."

Odessa and Lauren didn't look anything alike, but each woman had claimed her own beauty. At five-feet-three Lauren was delicate and fragile, her body softly curving and feminine. Her skin held the sensual deep browns of sable and mocha, reflecting a natural sheen of good health. Her large eyes sparkled like polished jet, mirroring her ebullient personality, and like Odessa's Lauren's short hair was expertly coiffed and the overall result was a quiet, deceptive beauty.

Odessa patted Lauren's cheek. "You've done well by the boy, sweetheart."

Lauren pulled away from her mother, staring at the small bird perched on the railing of the wraparound porch. "He's my life."

"Will you ever make room for someone else, Lauren?"

Lauren ran a hand through her own hair, sighing. She wondered why her mother had waited this long to bring up the subject of her not dating or trying to secure a husband. Odessa usually began the moment she stepped out of her car, because there was nothing that the two women could not discuss openly with each other.

"Not now. I'm too busy."

"You're too busy, Lauren? When you go to bed at night—alone—are you too busy to feel lonely? You're only twenty-seven. Why have you elected to spend your life denying your femininity?"

Lauren stood up and walked over to the steps. She sat down on the top one, feeling Odessa's gaze boring into her back. "I don't deny I have physical urges," she confessed.

"But do you do anything about them?" Odessa questioned.

She propped her elbows on her knees, shaking her head. "No, I don't."

"Why not, Lauren?"

Confusion filled Lauren's dark eyes. Her expression was strained, somber. Flashes of an island, a week of frivolity, came back with sharp clarity as her lids fluttered. Images of a couple, a man and a woman, tawny-brown and sleek sable-hued limbs blending and writhing in unbridled passion on a large bed, washed over her.

"Why not?" Odessa repeated.

Lauren's shoulders slumped. "Because I'm not looking for a husband."

Odessa left the love seat and sat down beside Lauren, unmindful that she wore raw silk slacks. "It doesn't have to be the way it was before, sweetheart. You were so young, so inexperienced."

"I was twenty-two and experienced enough, Mama."

Odessa's arms curved around Lauren's slim waist. "You may have been experienced, but certainly not worldly."

"That still doesn't change the fact that I should've never married Caleb Samuels."

"If that was the only way for me to get my grandson, then I'm glad you married Caleb Samuels," Odessa stated firmly. "But because you're a single mother it doesn't mean that you have to stop living. You're bright and you're gorgeous. Men should be wearing out the grass beating a path to this place."

Lauren managed a smile. "You're quite biased, Mama."

Odessa tilted her chin. "I have to be. You're a part of me. And you're my only child."

Lauren kissed Odessa's cheek. "I love you." Her eyes crinkled in laughter. "I'm going to make you a promise. As soon as Drew is in school I'm going to go out and get involved in some local organizations."

Odessa did not look convinced. "Does Andrew Monroe have anything to do with you not seeing other men?"

Shifting, Lauren stared at her mother. She knew Odessa always spoke her mind, but this was the first time she had ever mentioned the possibility that she thought Lauren was involved with Andrew.

"Andrew is my agent," Lauren stated in a voice laced with repressed annoyance.

Odessa ignored Lauren's indignant tone. "But does he want to be more than your agent, Lauren? Perhaps he wants to be your lover. Or better yet, your husband and a father to Drew?"

Lauren rose to her feet, brushing off the seat of her shorts. "Andrew will never be more to me than what he is now. And that is my agent and my friend."

Odessa stood up, towering above Lauren by four inches. "Don't misunderstand me. I like Andrew, Lauren."

"So do I, Mama. But not that way," she declared, waving at the mail carrier.

The mail carrier returned her wave, holding up a large envelope. An overnight envelope usually meant a check from Andrew. The last packet of research he had sold for her had earned him a sizeable commission.

"Good morning, Lauren," he called out as he made his

way up the path to the house. "Wonderful weather we're having."

Bright sun glinted off Frank Burton's orange-red hair. Working outdoors and without a hat had turned his delicate skin the same fiery red as his hair.

Frank handed Lauren the envelope and a pen, nodding at Odessa. "Good morning, ma'am."

Odessa gave him her best smile. "Good morning."

Lauren glanced at the return address on the mailing label as she scrawled her signature across the receipt. She was surprised to see the letter was not from Andrew.

Frank took his copy of the receipt, flashing a toothy grin. "Have a good day, ladies."

"You too," Lauren and Odessa chorused in unison.

Odessa watched Lauren open the mail, then extract a smaller white envelope. "Who's it from?" she asked, noting Lauren's puzzled expression.

"It's from a Boston law firm."

Odessa looked over Lauren's shoulder. "Is someone suing you?"

Lauren slid a finger under the flap. "I hope not." No one would ever sue her directly; she was a researcher and Andrew Monroe agented her work.

Her eyes quickly scanned the single sheet of type, rereading the words and not believing what she had read. Her legs were trembling as she sank down to the porch step, the paper fluttering to the ground.

Odessa caught her daughter's shoulders as she supported her head against a column. "What's the matter, baby?"

Lauren felt as if she had been transported back in time. It was mid-June, but then it could have been that brutally cold day in December when she and Caleb returned to Boston after a week-long stay on a private Caribbean island and she told him she no longer wanted to be married.

Icy fingers of fear had crept up her legs and lodged in

her chest when she remembered Cal's expression. The fear had seized her heart, not permitting her to draw a normal breath. Now that same fear had returned.

"He knows, Mama," she mumbled. Her worst nightmare had surfaced.

"He who, Lauren?" Odessa could not disguise the hysteria in her voice.

"Cal knows."

"You're not making sense, Lauren."

Lauren paused to catch her breath. "There's going to be a reading of Dr. Caleb Samuels's will and I've been summoned to attend."

"What does that mean?"

Lauren closed her eyes, reliving the old man's face. Cal had brought her to meet his grandfather the day they returned to the States. She had spent one night under the elderly man's roof, seeing his censuring glares before she realized she had been too impulsive, that she shouldn't have married his grandson.

"It means that the late Dr. Caleb Samuels must have uncovered that I had given birth to his great-grandson."

Odessa put her hands on her hips. "How? And if so, why didn't he acknowledge Drew while he was still alive?"

Lauren reopened her eyes. "I don't know. But I do know that Cal will be at the reading of the will."

"And you're going to attend. You have to, Lauren," Odessa insisted, seeing her daughter's impassive expression. "It's not for you, but Drew. You owe that to your little boy. He has a right to know who his father is."

"Let's not talk about rights." No one protected her right to choose when Cal took advantage of her vulnerability.

"But Caleb Samuels is Drew's father, and he has a right to know that he has a son."

"What will it all prove? Cal is as much a stranger to me as he'll be to Drew. There's no need to disrupt three lives: mine, Drew's and Cal's."

Odessa gave Lauren a long, penetrating look. "I think you're the only one who would be upset by all of this. It's going to come back to haunt you one of these days when Drew finds out that he could have had a relationship with his biological father but didn't because his mother didn't want to reopen an old wound. A wound too painful to bear."

"But Cal hates me, Mama. What if he wants Drew for himself? He hates me enough to fight for his son. I can't take that chance."

Odessa kissed Lauren's forehead. "I doubt that, sweetheart. Women don't lose their children that easily—even if the child's father is Caleb Samuels. And you can't take the chance that you won't lose Drew when he discovers years from now that you kept him from his father."

Lauren felt the tightness easing in her chest. "I know you're right. Deep down in my heart I know you're saying all of the right words."

"Don't listen to me. Think of Drew, then think of yourself. You've grown up with both of your parents. Isn't Drew entitled to that?"

"Cal lives in Spain," Lauren argued.

"Then perhaps Drew can spend his summers in Spain with his father."

"No!"

Odessa released Lauren and rose to her feet. She knew her daughter well enough not to press her. "Think about it, Lauren. I'll call you later."

Lauren sat on the porch step long after Odessa had driven away. She tried not thinking of the curve life had thrown her. One step forward, two steps backwards, and like it had happened one December day, Caleb Samuels would walk back into her life and change her forever. Only this time she would be prepared for him.

* * *

"Good morning. I'm Lauren Taylor. I have an appointment with Mr. Evans for ten."

The secretary offered Lauren a friendly smile. "Good morning, Miss Taylor. Mr. Evans will be with you shortly. You're to have a seat in the conference room. This way please."

Lauren followed the secretary up a flight of carpeted stairs in the elegantly appointed two-story building. She was shown into a spacious conference room with paneled walls and exquisite reproductions of pictures.

"Would you like a cup of coffee or tea, Miss Taylor?" the secretary asked.

"No—no thank you," Lauren replied, unable to pull her gaze away from the man seated at the oaken conference table.

Cal Samuels held back his surprise, rose to his feet, circled the table and pulled out a chair for Lauren in a show of civility, of politeness. It was as if nothing had happened; as if he had never met Lauren Taylor; as if they had never laughed, loved and married.

"Thank you," Lauren mumbled softly. He lingered over her head, inhaling the scent of her perfume, his warm breath increasing the heat in her face.

Cal straightened, moving away, and retook his own seat. An inner strength he never knew he possessed permitted him to affect his air of indifference while every nerve in his body screamed rage and frustration.

Seeing Lauren, being so close to her, threatened to break the fragile hold on his iron-willed control. He fixed his gaze on her small hands, recalling the heavy weight of his ring on her delicate finger.

His gaze returned to her face, and he was shocked by the full impact of her mature beauty. The little girl in a woman's body was gone; the naïveté in her large, expressive dark eyes was missing, and the waiflike slimness of her petite body had also vanished.

Everything he had remembered about her had disappeared and was replaced by a woman so hypnotically beautiful that for a brief second he was blind to her deceit.

He had loved her; he had offered her his life and his protection and she had thrown both back in his face.

I don't think I want to be married—not to you—not to anyone.

Her parting words were branded in his brain. He would carry them to his grave. Staring openly at her, Cal realized Lauren was alluring and much more composed than she had ever been five years before.

He hadn't thought he would ever see her again, and he wondered why she had been summoned to the reading of his grandfather's will.

Lauren returned Cal's bold stare. He was graying prematurely. She wondered how old he was now—thirty-three or thirty-four? Staring at him, she saw more changes. He wore his hair closer-cut than he had when they married. His tawny skin was darker, bronzed by the Mediterranean wind and sun.

However, his eyes had not changed. They were still brilliant amber fires. But now they appeared more yellow than gold. She studied his face, feature by feature, noting that age had given Caleb Samuels a masculine sensuality not seen on many men.

She dropped her gaze. What unnerved her more than seeing Caleb Samuels again was the realization of how much Drew resembled his father. Drew had inherited Cal's angular face, black curling hair, high forehead and strong jaw. The little boy was an exact replica of Caleb Baldwin Samuels II.

The silence between them was smothering, deafening in its thickness. Cal's expression was grim as he watched her and Lauren was overwhelmed with the anguish stirring within her; she had lied to herself—over and over. Even when she knew it, she still lied. The knowledge twisted in her until she wanted to shout out that she loved him—had always loved him.

The door to the conference room opened and the cloying scent of an expensive perfume wafted through the space as a tall woman strode in. This time Cal was slower in rising to his feet when he glared at the woman dressed in black linen with a vibrant Valentino scraf draped casually over one shoulder. Her body was lush, her face a perfect oval, and she carried herself confidently, seemingly aware of the appreciative glances that followed her.

"Good morning, Caleb," she drawled. Her voice was low and hard, belying her curvaceous body and pampered face.

"Is it, Jacqueline?" he returned, his eyes blazing with an unnamed emotion.

Lauren watched Cal and the woman, feeling their tension. The woman was older than Cal, but not by much.

The woman Cal had addressed as Jacqueline gave him a sensual smile. "Of course it is, darling." She slid gracefully onto a chair. "After the reading of your grandfather's will we'll never have to see each other again." Cal sat down, his mouth tightening.

A pregnant silence ensued, Lauren staring at Cal, he staring at Lauren and Jacqueline throwing glares at Cal and Lauren. It was apparent there were bad feelings between Cal and Jacqueline and Lauren was certain Cal's hostility also extended to her because if his grandfather knew about Drew she was certain he also knew about his son, and she wondered why he hadn't asked her about the child.

She hadn't tried to contact Cal after their marriage was annulled and she discovered herself pregnant—there was no way she was going to beg him to take her back because she was carrying his child; but if Cal had come after her asking that she give their marriage a chance she would've fallen into his arms and begged for forgiveness. But he did not come and she did not tell him that he had a son.

Nervously, Lauren crossed her legs under the table, smoothing out the slim skirt to her white silk dress. Unlike Cal and Jacqueline, she had selected pale colors: a white

Rochelle Alers

wrap dress with a shawl collar, white ostrich-skin pumps and matching shoulder bag. The color was the perfect foil for her clear sable-brown skin tones.

The door opened and closed a final time. A man entered, cradling a folder under his arm. He took a chair at the head of the table.

His eyes were friendly behind the lenses of his glasses. His thinning hair was cut close, while he had compensated for his hair loss by affecting a neat beard.

"I'm John Evans," he began in a soothing, professional tone, "and I'm responsible for handling the legal work on Dr. Caleb Samuels's estate." He opened the file folder. "Miss Taylor?" Lauren nodded in acknowledgement. "Mrs. Samuels and Mr. Samuels."

Lauren's pulses raced and she wondered if Jacqueline was Cal's wife. She sucked in her breath slowly, then let it out, and for the first time since she'd received the letter from Barlow, Mann and Evans, she questioned her sanity. What was she doing here?

It's not for me; it's for Drew, she'd told herself and continued to do so. Her mind wandered when John Evans began reading from several typed pages in the file. She forced herself to concentrate on what he was saying.

"Dr. Samuels had our firm draw up what is considered a simple will," John continued. "His estate will be divided into three equal shares, the first going to his alma mater, Fisk University. A contribution of one million dollars has been designated to build the Dr. Caleb B. Samuels Academic Center from the proceeds of the sale of land of family holdings in Mississippi, Alabama and Georgia, originally deeded to Elias, Marcus and Jefferson Samuels, dated eighteen eighty-three, eighty-five and eighty-nine respectively. This contribution will be used to increase classroom space and house a research center dedicated to the study of African-American history.

"A gift of one million dollars from awards, including the Nobel Prize for Medicine, will be bestowed to St.

Martin's Hospital for their continuing research efforts in sickle cell anemia."

Three pairs of eyes were trained on the attorney. Lauren felt John Evans was saving the best for last. She glanced down at Jacqueline Samuels's clenched fingers. The band of diamonds on the third finger of her right hand glittered in contrast to her smooth umber coloring.

"Dr. Samuels has bequeathed the remainder of his estate to his great-grandson Drew Michael Taylor-Samuels."

"What!" Jacqueline screamed, bolting from her chair.

"Please, Mrs. Samuels," John pleaded.

Jacqueline recovered quickly, retaking her seat and smoothing back her straightened hair. "I'm sorry, Mr. Evans. It's just that it has come as a shock to hear that Dr. Samuels has a great-grandchild." She shot Cal a withering look then turned her wild-eyed gaze on Lauren.

"Just who the hell are you anyway? You don't look like *his* type," she said, frowning and marring her almost too-beautiful face.

Cal's eyes raked Lauren like fired citrines as his chest rose and fell heavily under the crisp front of his white shirt. Seeing Lauren again had robbed him of speech, and in its place was repressed rage. Now he knew why Lauren had been summoned to the law office. She had had his child. She had kept his son from him. She had compounded her deceit by not letting him know that he was a father.

"I'd like to continue, Mrs. Samuels," the attorney admonished in a velvet tone.

Jacqueline shifted her eyebrows. "Please do."

"There is proof that this child Drew Michael Taylor-Samuels is the issue of Dr. Samuels's grandson Caleb Baldwin Samuels II and Miss Lauren Vernice Taylor."

There was no doubt about Drew's paternity, Cal thought. Lauren was the only woman he had ever slept with, whom he deliberately wanted to get pregnant.

"What kind of stunt are you two trying to pull off?" Jacqueline gasped. She turned to Lauren. "You scheming little thief! You conspired with this piece of slime to cheat me out of what is due me."

Cal was galvanized into action. His open hand came down hard on the table, the sound resembling the crack of a rifle. "Watch your mouth, Jacqueline," he warned in a dangerously soft voice.

She half rose to her feet. "Or you'll what, Caleb?"

John Evans stood up. "Please, please. Try to restrain yourselves. I'd like to conclude this as soon as possible."

"Oh, there's more, Counselor," Jacqueline sneered.

John nodded. "Yes, Mrs. Samuels, there's more."

"Well, let's hear the rest of this bull," Jacqueline mumbled angrily.

John straightened his tie and sat down. "A trust fund will be set up in the name of Drew Michael Taylor-Samuels in the sum of one million dollars. Drew Michael Taylor-Samuels will be eligible to withdraw the sum total of one hundred thousand dollars each year, commencing with the anniversary of his twenty-first birthday.

"Drew Michael Taylor-Samuels will be entitled to this privilege with the proviso his parents Caleb Baldwin Samuels II and Lauren Vernice Taylor marry and share a common domicile within sixty days of the reading of this will, and shall remain married for a period of not less than one year. Failure to marry or to maintain a common domicile for the specified time stipulated by the terms of this document will nullify this clause and the proceeds are transferable to Jacqueline Harvell Samuels by default."

A smile played around the corners of Cal's mouth as he crossed his arms over his chest. Even though his mouth was smiling, his eyes were hard and cold.

"The sly old fox," Jacqueline mumbled softly, shaking her head. "He holds out the carrot, then snatches it back. I've always hated that heartless old bastard."

John Evans closed the folder. "Does everyone understand the terms of this will?"

Lauren understood it—too well, but that did not mean she would agree to the terms. There was no way she was going to let Dr. Samuels control her, not even from his grave.

A million dollars was a lot of money for Drew. More than she could ever hope to earn in her lifetime. She chewed her lower lip, frowning slightly. But what if Drew wanted to become a doctor like his great-grandfather? Would she be able to afford the cost of medical school without securing loans? Probably not, however she wasn't willing to tempt fate by permitting Cal in her life again. She had no intention of marrying Cal again just so that her son could inherit someone else's money.

Cal rose to his feet, resplendent in a lightweight navy blue summer suit. Lauren had almost forgotten his towering height and how well he wore his clothes. An even six-foot, Cal had managed to remain trim. She felt her face heat up when she realized she was quite familiar with his body—with and without his clothing, in and out of bed.

Jacqueline opened her purse and withdrew an enameled compact. She checked her face and snapped it shut. Running her tongue over her front teeth, she glanced up at Cal. "When's the wedding, Caleb?"

His gaze was fixed on Lauren's face. "Next month, Jacqueline," he replied, his eyes narrowing. Somehow Cal had forgotten Lauren's diminutive height, her petite body, the satiny feel of her flawless dark brown skin and the delicate feminine scent that was hers and hers alone. But he hadn't forgotten her passion. A passion so wild and so intense that he had not wanted to lose it once he found it. He would have given up everything he had, rather than give up Lauren Taylor-Samuels.

Jacqueline's expertly arched brows shifted as she watched Cal staring at Lauren, and for the first time since she had entered the room she visually assessed the mother of Cal's child. Lauren may not have been the type of woman Jacqueline had known Cal to consort with, but she did recognize something about Lauren Taylor most men would find irresistible: a little-girl innocence coupled with an overriding desire to protect her.

"Am I invited to the wedding . . . what is your name again, little girl?"

Lauren's head spun around. She did not know Jacqueline Samuels, and she did not want to, but there was something about the woman she disliked on sight. "It's Miss Taylor. And no you're not invited. It's going to be a private ceremony."

Jacqueline quickly assessed an obduracy in Lauren Taylor that wasn't apparent at first glance, and concluded the younger woman would not be an easy opponent. Gathering her purse, she said, "I don't mind not celebrating your wedding, but I'll sure enjoy its demise."

Jacqueline did not see the hateful glare Cal gave Lauren as she leaned over and patted Lauren's shoulder. "Good luck, little girl. You're going to need it to survive a year with the high and mighty Caleb Samuels. He's just a younger version of the heartless old bastard he was named for."

She walked out of the room and John Evans offered Lauren a conciliatory smile. "If there's anything I can help you with, please let me know," he said.

Lauren stood up, extending a small slender hand. "Thank you very much. I have your card."

He grasped her hand, released her fingers, then turned to Cal. "You know where to find me."

Cal took the proffered hand. "Thanks again, John."

John winked at him. "Good luck," he returned softly.

Cal waited until John walked out of the conference room, then circled the table. He stood over Lauren like a messenger of death, his gaze drilling her to the spot. "You and I have to talk. Perhaps you can enlighten me on this child I'm supposed to have fathered." The fingers of his right hand closed around her upper arm.

Lauren had never denied her child, and she was not going to begin now. Not even to his father.

"You have a son," she replied through clenched teeth.

Cal's expression did not change. "So I've been told. Why did I have to wait until today to hear about it?"

Lauren's eyes widened as she stared at Cal in astonishment. "But . . . but didn't you know?"

His golden stare drilled into her. "No."

"But your grandfather knew."

"He knew and you knew. Everyone knew except *me.*"

Her mind reeled in confusion. Why wouldn't Dr. Samuels tell Cal that he was a father?

Cal thrust his face close to her, so close she saw a light sheen of moisture on his upper lip. Close enough to note the tiny pores in his golden-brown skin. So close she could smell his after-shave mingling with his own personal masculine scent when she felt the heat of his breath and his rage.

"Who put you up to this? How did you con my grandfather?"

Lauren pulled her arm from his loose grip, snatching up her handbag. "Who are you angry with, Cal? It can't be me because I get nothing out of this deal. If you want or need the money that badly, why don't you seduce Jacqueline. She's still young enough to give you a son. That way you both can keep the money in the *family.*" She turned and walked out of the conference room.

"Lauren!" Cal shouted after her.

She did not stop. She ignored the receptionist's smile, pushing open the front door and stepping out into the bright summer sun.

Lauren made it to her car in the parking lot, but could not escape. A large hand captured hers in an iron grip.

"I said we have to talk," Cal hissed close to her ear.

Lauren stared at his hand holding her captive. "Let me go."

Cal loosened his grip, but he would not permit Lauren to escape him as he trapped her between her car and his body.

"I want to talk to you."

Lauren tilted her chin. "There's nothing to talk about."

He moved closer, pressing his chest against her shoulder. "That's where you're wrong, Lauren Taylor-Samuels. You and I have a great deal to discuss."

"It's Lauren Taylor. I'd stopped being Samuels years ago, you arrogant . . ."

Cal's frown vanished. "And you agreed to marry me and all of my arrogance," he countered with a hint of a smile.

Some of the defensiveness seemed to flow out of Lauren with his smile. He was right. She had agreed to marry him, aware of his celebrity status, the rumors surrounding his sybaritic lifestyle and his infuriating arrogance.

His lids lowered over the golden eyes with their dark brown centers. "I want to know about my son, Lauren."

Lauren's gaze went from his face to her hand. He released her, stepping back. "What is it you want to know, Cal?"

"Not here," he said.

A slight frown furrowed her forehead. "Where?"

"At my grandfather's house. You can follow in your car."

He left her, walking over to a sleek black sports car, not giving her the opportunity to protest. She waited until he had slipped behind the wheel and started up the motor before she opened the door to her own mid-size car.

Cal pulled alongside her, leaning over to the passenger side. "Try to keep up," he was shouting over the hum of the two engines.

"I don't speed, Cal."

Lauren could have been talking to herself as she

watched the exhaust from Cal's car. She lost him at a light, forcing him to slow down and wait for her.

Unbidden, she remembered his high-speed driving along the narrow roads on Cay Verde. Sitting in the car with Cal, watching his long fingers shift gears, had given her a rush; a rush that matched the uncontrollable soaring she experienced when they had made love; a rush so indelibly engraved in her consciousness that she had not sought out another man to see if it could be duplicated.

Lauren slowed her car even more, and when Cal parked in front of the three-story town house she knew he was enraged.

He was out of his car, slamming the door violently before she shut off her engine. "Where did you buy your license?" he snapped, leaning into the open window.

Lauren rolled up the window and pushed open the door, forcing him to move quickly to avoid injury. "I said I don't speed. I'm used to driving with a child, and I intend to live long enough to raise that child."

Cal pushed his hands into the pockets of his trousers. He smiled broadly. "My son?"

"No, my son."

He sobered quickly, the smile fading. "Is he or is he not my son, Lauren?"

"You may have fathered him, but he is my son. Don't ever forget that, Caleb."

Cal studied Lauren, recognizing an inner strength he had missed at the law office. This petite woman—one he had loved and married—had carried and given birth to his son; the son he had prayed for; the son he had not known existed until today.

He extended a hand and pulled Lauren to her feet. "Let's go inside."

Chapter Two

Cal led Lauren through the entry and living room, then into the same library where she had first met the late Dr. Caleb Samuels in what now seemed so very long ago. Most of the furniture was covered with dust covers.

She felt as if she had stepped back in time where she could see the elderly man rising to his feet to greet his grandson with his new bride. The old man's dark eyes had blazed fire; a fire that seemed to pierce her stoic facade to see her fear when she realized how capricious she had been to marry Cal Samuels.

And that brief meeting with Dr. Samuels had been the catalyst to shock Lauren back to reality. She had made a mistake to marry—especially if that man was best-selling author C. B. Samuels.

Cal slipped out of his jacket, extracted the cuff links and rolled his shirt cuffs back over strong brown wrists.

"Please be seated." He waved a hand toward a chair. "Can I get you anything to drink?"

Lauren sat, crossing one leg over the other. "No thank you. I'd like to get this over so I can return home."

Cal studied her relaxed position. "Where's home?"

She waited until he removed a covering from a love seat and sat down before saying, "Grafton. North Grafton to be precise."

"How long have you lived there?"

"Two months."

"Do you like it?" Cal continued with his questioning.

"Very much. Look, Caleb. I . . ."

"About the child," he interrupted.

"Drew."

Cal nodded, closing his eyes. The sunlight pouring through heavy red damask drapes glinted off the silver in his hair, creating a halo effect.

Lauren felt a wave of uneasiness shake her. She did not think she would be so unnerved by seeing Caleb Samuels again, and she called on all of her reserves to deal with this flesh-and-blood man sitting three feet from her.

He was not a man a woman could forget easily. Meeting Caleb Samuels shocked and assaulted one's senses. Everything about him: his fluid walk, soft voice and his controlled personality. Lauren was surprised with his outburst at Jacqueline during the reading of the will.

"Drew," he repeated softly. He opened his eyes. "Why didn't you let me know about the child?"

"Why didn't your grandfather tell you?" Lauren retorted, answering his question with one of her own.

"It wasn't my grandfather's responsibility to tell me, Lauren."

"You know why I couldn't tell you."

Cal's jaw hardened as his eyes widened. "I don't know, Lauren. Perhaps you should tell me."

She chewed her lower lip, composing her thoughts. "I didn't find out that I was pregnant until after the annulment."

Cal leaned forward on his chair. "Not being married is not a factor when there is a child. I had a right to know there was a child."

Lauren knew he was right, and she floundered before his brilliant stare, huddling in her chair and offering no response.

Cal sucked in his breath, cursing to himself as he registered vulnerability in Lauren for the first time. He also shared the blame. He was equally guilty because he should have fought for her. He shouldn't have given in to her when she wanted to leave him. He still loved her; there was never a time since she had left him when he did not love her, and he realized now why his grandfather had not told him about the child. The elder Samuels thought if Cal didn't fight to hold on to his wife he would not have fought for his son.

"How old is he, Lauren?"

Lauren felt her throat tighten. There was no mistaking the pain in Cal's voice. This was not the Cal she remembered. When she'd told him she was leaving him, he showed no emotion. He merely nodded and she walked out on him.

"He'll turn four on September first."

"Does he know about me?"

"I've tried explaining that you don't live in this country."

Cal sat up straighter. "Does he know my name?"

"No."

"Why not?" he fired back.

"I didn't want to confuse him."

A sudden icy contempt flared in his eyes. "What were you going to tell him five or ten years from now, Lauren? Would you be able to come up with an excuse good enough to make up for your forgetting to tell me that I had fathered a child, and that I wasn't allowed to be a father to that child?"

She wanted to refute his accusation, but could not. Her delicate jaw tightened as she glared at him. "It wouldn't have come to that."

"Why not?"

"Because I would've told Drew the truth."

"I'll tell him the truth when I see him."

Lauren was so enraged she could hardly speak. "You won't."

"That's where you're wrong, Lauren. I will see my son and we will marry—again."

Lauren felt as if Cal had caught her by the throat, not permitting her to escape. "Never," she croaked.

"I want my son, Lauren."

She felt her temper rise in response to his demand. "You'll get to see your son, but I . . ."

"I want my son and you," he insisted, cutting her off.

Lauren clenched her teeth. "I'm not going to marry you, Cal. I don't make the same mistake twice."

A tense silence enveloped the room as Cal lowered his chin and looked up at her from lowered lids. "I'd marry anyone to keep Jacqueline from getting another penny of my family's money. My stepmother destroyed my father and I'll be damned if she's going to make a mockery of his memory by inheriting my grandfather's legacy."

Lauren refused to relent. "Jacqueline Samuels is your problem, not mine."

"She's Drew's problem now."

"Leave Drew out of this."

"I won't, Lauren. Drew is the reason you're in Boston this morning. Drew is the reason we're having this conversation."

"I'm not going to let you use my son for your personal vendetta."

Cal shook his head, giving her a smug grin. "I thought he was *our* son."

She felt properly chastised. "Okay, Caleb, *our* son."

"I can't turn back the clock," Cal stated, crossing his arms over his chest. "Neither of us can, but I can make certain Drew will get what's rightfully his. His name may be Taylor, but he's also a Samuels."

After a long pause, Lauren asked, "What's this all about, Cal? Is it about money or is it about revenge?"

"It's about family. Whether you want to acknowledge it, Drew is family. The same way you were once family. My family."

"It's more like manipulation," she retorted angrily. "A dead man is manipulating our lives from his grave, and I want no part of it."

Cal concealed a smile. "If that's the case, why did you tell Jacqueline that she wasn't invited to our wedding?"

Lauren compressed her lips into a tight line. "I don't like people who call me a thief."

"Nothing you could say to Jacqueline could hurt her as much as your being Drew's mother."

Lauren's gaze was fixed on the toe of her shoe and she missed Cal's slow, seductive approval of her shapely legs in the heels. He had only glimpsed the natural grace and beauty waiting to flourish with her ripening womanhood when he first saw her on Cay Verde before he realized there was a mysterious spirit within Lauren that captured his heart.

He wanted his son, but he wanted Lauren more.

"When can I meet Drew?" he asked, startling her.

Lauren's head jerked up. She knew there was no way she could keep Cal from meeting Drew. No court of law would deny him his child, and it seemed as if she had waited years for this scenario.

"I'll call you," she replied calmly even though her heart was pounding and slamming against her ribs.

"When?" His voice was soft and gentle. Despite Lauren's deceit, Cal did not want to hurt her.

"Maybe tomorrow. I have to talk to Drew first."

"Where do you want to meet?"

"You can come out to the house."

They had reached a truce—an uneasy truce in spite of their very stubborn natures. Drew would meet his father, and even though Lauren still loved Cal she had no intention of ever remarrying him, regardless of the stipulations in Dr. Samuels's will.

Cal moved from the love seat and held out a hand to Lauren. He smiled when she placed her hand in his. "It's going to be all right, Lauren. I won't **fight** you for the child."

She gave him a tremulous smile. "Thank you, Cal."

His hands slipped up her arms, pulling her closer. He studied her face, feature by feature, trying to see if there were remnants of the woman-child he had married.

Her hair was different. What had been a simple page-boy was now stylishly cut short, the top full and curling and the sides tapered to frame her small face.

He gazed deeply into her large dark eyes, drowning in the black pools. A familiar stirring flooded his body and he released her.

"I'll walk you to your car." There was an edge to his voice he could not control. He wanted her; he would always want her.

Lauren schooled her features not to reveal the desire pulsing throughout her body. She still had not gotten Caleb Samuels out of her system. It had been a long time—too long and yet she was powerless to resist him.

"You'll need my telephone number," Cal reminded her, walking over to a table. He wrote down a number on a pad near a telephone. Turning back to her, he handed her the sheet of paper. "I'll wait here for the call."

Lauren nodded and placed the paper in her handbag. Together they made their way to the front door.

Cal escorted her down the steps and took the keys from her hand. Unlocking her car door, he held it open until she slid behind the wheel. His gaze lingered on the expanse of silken leg and thigh when she sat down. Dropping the keys into her outstretched palm, he smiled.

"Don't drive too fast," he teased.

Lauren couldn't help laughing. The sound was natural and carefree, surprising both of them. "I won't."

Cal leaned in through the open window. "Call me," he ordered softly.

"I will," she confirmed.

Lauren's gaze was fixed on his mouth, her dark eyes

caressing his full upper lip. It gave him the look of a petulant little boy. But she knew Caleb Samuels was anything but a little boy.

She turned on the ignition and Cal took several steps back to the sidewalk. Flipping her directional signal, Lauren glanced over her shoulder then pulled away from the curb with a scream of rubber hitting the roadway.

Peering up in the rearview mirror, she smiled. Cal's expression was one of mixed surprise and shock. She took the next corner slowly, turning down the street that would take her to her parents' house.

"How did it go?" Odessa asked after Lauren had kicked off her shoes and raised her stockinged feet to a chintz-covered ottoman on the sun porch.

Lauren's brow furrowed. "It was weird, crazy. No, Mama, it was bizarre."

"How?"

A half-smile played at the corners of Lauren's mouth as she related the terms and conditions of the late Dr. Caleb B. Samuels's will. "All I have to do is marry Cal, live with him for a year and Drew will inherit in excess of one million dollars. That will include the interest it'll earn until Drew's twenty-one."

Now it was Odessa's turn to frown. "What I don't understand is how Dr. Samuels found out about Drew when you didn't tell him."

Lauren shook her head. "He must have had someone investigate me."

"And Cal didn't know?"

"He said he didn't know."

"Do you believe him, Lauren?"

Lauren remembered Cal's expression when John Evans revealed Drew's existence. There was no way Cal could've faked his reaction.

"Yes, I do."

"But why wouldn't Dr. Samuels tell Cal about Drew?"

Lauren pressed her head against the fluffy cushioned back of the rocker. "We'll never know. The dead don't tell tales." She pursed her lips. "I suspect Dr. Samuels wanted to pay me back for walking out on Cal."

"I take it Cal wants to meet his son?" Odessa continued with her questioning. Lauren nodded. "When and where will this take place?"

Lauren felt as if a weight had been lifted from her mind and body. Even though she had not thought it would ever happen, she had mentally prepared herself for the inevitable. Someday, sometime and somewhere Drew would meet his father.

"Probably tomorrow." She noted her mother's strained expression. "I'm going to talk to Drew tonight, then I'll call Cal tomorrow. I think it's best that Cal come to Drew rather than Drew go to him."

"I agree with you," Odessa concurred. "Now, how about you, sweetheart? How was it seeing Caleb Samuels again?"

Lauren had always maintained an open rapport with her mother, telling her things most daughters balked at disclosing; but how could she tell Odessa that what she had felt for Cal that wildly passionate week on Cay Verde was still alive. That she wanted to relive that week again—over and over.

"It went rather smoothly," she said instead. "Time has been kind to Cal even though he's a little more gray."

Odessa raised an eyebrow. "I asked about you, not Cal Samuels."

Lauren felt her face heat up. She had given away her feelings for Cal. "I'm still attracted to him, Mama," she confessed.

For once, Odessa decided not to press her daughter about her relationship with Caleb Samuels, recognizing Lauren's need to come to grips with the legal proceedings she had encountered earlier that morning.

"What about the money willed to Drew?" she asked.

"What about it, Mama? Someone mentions money and all of the sharks begin circling around the wounded prey, measuring for the final kill. Drew will not become that prey if I have anything to say about it."

Odessa rose to her feet, glaring down at Lauren. "Why is it always what *you* want?"

Turning her back, Lauren compressed her lips in a tight, angry line. Her mother was being pushy again. "Because he is my child, and I will always do what is best for my child."

Odessa reached for Lauren's arm, spinning her around. "It's time you started thinking of others, Lauren. You're not in this by yourself. Drew loves you, but you'd better get used to the possibility that once he meets his father he'll love him also." Her fingers grazed Lauren's cheek. "You're going to have to share your son with Caleb and whatever Caleb has to offer him.

"I want you to think of your son, darling," Odessa continued softly. She smiled seductively. "I'm also certain you can think of worse things than waking up in bed with Caleb Samuels."

Lauren laughed, her mouth softening. She felt desire sweep through her body when she thought about how it had been to share a bed with Cal.

"You're right about that, Mama."

"How much time do you have before Caleb's wicked stepmother can claim my grandson's legacy?"

"Sixty days," Lauren replied.

Odessa shrugged slender shoulders. "That's not too bad. The old despot could've said two weeks. That would've meant big trouble."

Lauren saw a mischievous glint in Odessa's clear brown eyes. "Stay out of this," Lauren warned in a soft voice. "If you even think about interfering . . ."

"You'll what, dear?" Odessa asked with a saccharine grin.

"I'll think of something."

"You're dangerous when you think, Lauren."

"Don't test me, Mother."

"Don't call me Mother."

"Just don't interfere."

"But, baby . . ." Odessa threw up her hands. "Okay. I promise I won't interfere."

Lauren hugged and kissed Odessa. "Thank you."

"Are you and Drew staying for lunch?"

Lauren gave her mother a loving smile. "Of course."

"Sit and relax," Odessa suggested. "I'll call you when lunch is ready."

Closing her eyes, Lauren willed her mind and body to relax. The warm summer breeze filtering through the screened windows cooled her and reminded her of the warm trade winds rustling the fronds of palm trees on Cay Verde.

She smiled. She had passed the test. She hadn't fallen under Cal's sensual spell again, and he had no way of knowing how much she had loved him and still loved him.

There had been many times since Lauren left Cal that she tried remembering what he looked like, what he had smelled like, and the rapturous pleasure he evoked when he kissed, touched and tasted her body.

Lauren had fallen in love with Caleb Samuels on Cay Verde and she would love him forever.

Cay Verde—a lovers' paradise. That's where it all began.

Chapter Three

Lauren had never heard of Cay Verde until she was summoned to meet with the head of Summit Publishing's research department a snowy December morning five years ago.

"How would you like to spend seven days on a private island in the Caribbean, Lauren?" Bob Ferguson had asked once she was seated.

Lauren's gaze had shifted from Bob to the wide window behind his desk. A shield of gray obscured the sky. Snow had been falling steadily all morning.

"What do I give up in return?" she'd questioned, smiling.

"The most comprehensive research ever gathered on the Zulu nation."

Lauren knew the Zulus were African tribal people of Bantu stock, tall and powerfully built, but her knowledge was limited to those few facts.

Bob explained that a book packager had come up with a series concept about the Zulu chieftain Shaka and his successors. He told Lauren the concept would be comparable in scope to the eight-book series of John Jakes's *The American Bicentennial Series,* and C. B. Samuels would be the major writer for the projected four-book series. Chiefs Shaka, Dingane, Mpande and Cetewayo would each have their stories, fusing historical facts with fictional accountings to produce what Summit predicted to be a potential blockbuster series.

Lauren was the newest and youngest researcher for Summit, but Bob Ferguson knew Lauren was also one of their best. Fortified with an excellent liberal arts background, she had been hired immediately after graduating from college and she'd been promoted several times within her first year. Her zeal and thoroughness in approaching each research project had caught his attention and every department head at Summit.

Lauren successfully controlled the torrent of excitement building within her. She was being offered a project most veteran researchers would gladly forfeit the many perks Summit offered its long-time employees.

Bob watched her impassive expression. "Before you make your decision, I think it's only fair to let you know that C. B. Samuels usually works very closely with his researcher, and he can be quite difficult when he doesn't get the facts he's requested."

Lauren had read about C. B. Samuels's volatile artistic temperament, but refused to let that thwart her. She was confident she would work well with the best-selling fiction writer.

"C. B. will live on Cay Verde until he completes the first book," Bob continued. "He'll then take a year off, return to Spain, then come back to Cay Verde to write the second book. After that he's contracted to give us the third and fourth books within three years."

"What's the projected word count?" Lauren asked.

"Three-hundred to five-hundred thousand."

A slight frown appeared between her eyes. Big books meant extensive research. Buoyed by a burst of confidence, she said, "I'll accept it."

Bob let out his breath in an audible sigh. An unconscious voice had told him Lauren Taylor would accept the project, but somehow he couldn't bring himself to believe it until now. He was afraid that C. B. Samuels's reputation would prompt Lauren to reject the assignment as other researchers had done.

"Be ready to leave in two days. I'll have my secretary make the arrangements for your flight. You'll also get a generous check for expenses. There'll be more than enough to cover the cost of a new wardrobe. I hear the nightlife on the island is quite festive," he added, winking.

Lauren's smile was dazzling. "Thanks, Bob."

"Don't thank me, Lauren. "You've earned this assignment."

"I'll do you proud." Her voice was low and filled with checked emotion.

Bob gave her a lingering look. "I know you will." He visually admired her tiny body as she stood up. "Call me once you get to Cay Verde," he said, also rising to his feet.

Lauren nodded and walked out of Robert Ferguson's office, her step light, her spirits soaring, ready for Cay Verde and C. B. Samuels.

Her flight to the Bahamas, then the connecting one in a small propeller plane to Cay Verde was uneventful and accomplished with a minimum of delay. Lauren arrived at noon, refreshed, ready to work and to enjoy the natural splendor of the island.

A driver, with a lilting island accent, acted as her tour guide, driving slowly along the major road and pointing out the sprawling residences belonging to the six families who had pooled their vast wealth and bought the island.

Lauren settled back against the aged leather seat in the vintage Mercedes convertible and reveled in the warm breezes caressing her face. Five hours earlier she had waited in Boston's Logan Airport, watching clouds race across a gunmetal-gray sky. Below-freezing temperatures had hinted of more snow.

"Here we are, missy," the driver announced.

He stopped in front of a large two-storied white stucco

structure that was truly West Indian in character, with a red Spanish-tiled roof, veranda, and Creole jalousie shutters. Exotic blooming flowers, banana trees and noisy brightly colored birds added to the property's lushness.

Lauren was helped from the car and escorted into the house where she was greeted by a young woman barely out of her teens.

"Welcome, Miss Taylor. I am Judith," she said. "I am here to help you for your stay on Cay Verde. Please come with me." Her accent was the same as the driver's, lending a musical sound to familiar words.

Lauren smiled at Judith and followed her up a flight of stairs to the second level. Her bedroom was large and filled with bright sunlight. A massive four-poster canopy bed of Jamaican mahogany was the focus of attention, along with a matching armoire and rocker. These were the only pieces of furniture in the expansive space.

Judith closed the shutters and turned on a ceiling fan. "I'll draw your bath, then I will unpack everything for you. I will also bring a platter of refreshments."

Lauren wanted to tell Judith she did not want anything to eat, but decided against it. She did not know the customs on Cay Verde and she didn't want to insult her absent host's hospitality or those in his employ.

An hour later, Lauren lay on the large bed, her head supported by fluffy pillows and fighting to keep her eyes open. The flight, the heat, and the platter of broiled fish, fresh fruit and rum-spiked punch had taken its toll. Giving into the languidness weighing on her limbs, she slept, and it wasn't until later that afternoon she met Caleb Samuels for the first time.

"Have you lost your mind? She looks as if she's not old enough to drink and you want this . . . this child . . . to do the research for this project!"

He had not shouted the words, but Caleb Samuels did

not have to. His intent was unmistakable. He did not want Lauren Taylor as his researcher.

"But Ferguson said she's the best," said a small, wiry man with glasses in a quiet voice.

"The best at what?" Caleb Samuels replied with a sneer, his eyes raking her body.

Lauren could not believe he would be that rude. Caleb Samuels had not bothered to hide his disdain.

"You don't have to like me," she countered, failing to control her quick temper and for the first time forgetting her position as a professional researcher. "But I am going to do the research on this project, Mr. Samuels; however if my youth offends you then I suggest we not communicate face to face. Modern technology has provided us with telephones and fax machines. Take your pick!" The blood pounded in her temples as she turned on her heel and walked away from the two men, not seeing the look of surprise on Caleb's face.

Lauren returned to her room and flopped across the bed, biting her lower lip and fighting back tears. She was angry at herself. She never should've allowed Caleb Samuels to bait her. She had fallen into his trap.

Inhaling, then letting out her breath slowly, Lauren vowed she would never lose her temper again—at least not with C. B. Samuels. She had to prove she was immune to his disparaging remarks, and conduct herself like the accomplished researcher she had become.

She left the bed, showered and changed her clothes for dinner. There was no way she was going to hide out in her room. Caleb Samuels would just have to get used to seeing her face.

Checking her watch, Lauren realized she had another hour before dinner was to be served. The dinner hour on Cay Verde usually began at nine and continued until eleven and sometimes as late as midnight. She decided to take a walk along the beach and she informed Judith she would be back in time for dinner.

Lauren made her way away from the house and down to the sea, carrying her sandals. The setting sun and cooler breezes refreshed her as she walked slowly along the beach, luxuriating in the beauty of the blue-green waters of the Caribbean quietly kissing the pure white sand.

Stopping, Lauren stared out at the large orange circle of the sun as it dipped lower and lower, meeting the uneven line of the sea, not seeing the figure of the man until he stood less than five feet from her.

The rays from the setting sun bathed him in flames, highlighting his tawny-brown skin and firing his golden eyes and turning his white attire a blazing red.

"I apologize for earlier today," he said in a voice so quiet Lauren had to strain to catch his words over the sound of the rustling sea. "It was rude of me . . ."

"It was arrogant of you," Lauren corrected. Cal smiled and she sucked in her breath. Earlier that afternoon she had been too incensed to note that Caleb Samuels was more attractive in person than his photographs revealed.

He bowed slightly at the waist. "I'm sorry for my arrogance, Miss Lauren Taylor, and to prove that I'm truly sorry I ask that you forget our prior encounter. Think of this as our first meeting."

Lauren brushed several strands of wind-blown hair away from her cheek, unaware of the delicate, sensual vision she presented Cal. He had called her a child, but she was anything but a child. A pale pink sheer voile sundress, with a matching underslip, flattered her petite figure. On her, the deep-V neckline and bared back was innocent, yet on a woman with a more voluptuous body it would have been seductive.

She was different; so different from the other women he had met that for a moment he felt like a tongue-tied boy. Lauren Taylor was a sexy woman-child with exquisite dark-brown velvet skin, large mysterious eyes and a passionate, succulent mouth that cried out to be kissed. She had the sexiest mouth of any woman he had ever seen.

He extended his right hand. "Cal Samuels," he said, finding his voice.

Lauren hesitated, then grasped the proffered hand. "Lauren Taylor."

Cal held her fingers gently, then released them. "Will you have dinner with me, Lauren?"

She was caught off guard by his unexpected invitation, but recovered quickly. "I can't, Mr. Samuels. You're much too old for me," she answered with a saccharine grin.

Cal's jaw dropped slightly as he ran a hand over his curling hair. "I know I'm graying prematurely, but I'm only twenty-eight."

Lauren resumed her walk along the beach, Cal falling in step with her. "You're still too old."

He glanced at her profile, enchanted by her fragile beauty. Her delicate features, soft feminine fragrance and her wide-eyed look of innocence charmed him.

"How old are you?" he questioned.

She smiled, giving him a sidelong glance. "Old enough to drink. I'm twenty-two."

"But . . . but I'm only six years older than you," he sputtered. "I hardly think that constitutes 'too old.' I'll be on my best behavior," he continued almost pleadingly, moving in front of her and impeding her progress. "I promise."

Lauren smiled up at him, watching his smile grow wider as he leaned toward her, realizing she was past the point of his intimidation. "Not tonight."

"When?" The single word held a hint of desperation.

"Tomorrow," she answered.

"Good morning, Lauren."

The soft male voice prompted Lauren to open her eyes

and she smiled up at the man looming over her, holding two cups of steaming coffee.

Bringing herself to a sitting position on the cushioned rattan lounge chair, she removed her sunglasses. She had awakened early and decided to sit under the sweeping leaves of a grove of banana trees to await breakfast.

"Good morning, Cal." Her smile was as dazzling as the bright sunshine.

Cal took a matching lounge chair, silently admiring Lauren's thick shiny hair, pulled off her face in a ponytail. She wore a body-hugging white tank top she had paired with a flowing white gauze cotton skirt.

He handed her a cup of coffee. "Judith said you like your coffee light with one sugar."

She smiled at him, taking the cup. "Thank you."

Lauren concentrated on her coffee instead of staring openly at Caleb Samuels. The man was so compelling, his magnetism so powerful that a delicious shudder of desire swept over her. She wasn't very worldly and hadn't had a lot of experience with the opposite sex, but the man sitting beside her projected a virility so intoxicating that she was helpless to resist it.

Lauren had never been one to believe the sordid supermarket tabloids, but she wondered if some of the rumors surrounding C. B. Samuels's licentious social life were true. It was hard for any normal female to resist his slim, tanned, hard brown body, curling graying black hair, brilliant sun-light eyes and pouting mouth, and when she had gone to bed the night before she tried remembering everything about him, including the sensual timbre of his soft voice.

Leaning back in his chair, Cal closed his eyes. "What do you know about the Zulus, Lauren?"

Lauren glanced at his bold profile. His expression was closed, as if he guarded a secret. "Not much," she admitted.

His mouth curved into a smile. "I think you're going to

have your work cut out for you with this project," he said and confirming that she would be his researcher.

"I want a lot of facts—detailed facts," he continued. "I want to know every historical event recorded about Shaka, his half-brother Dingane, Dingane's brother Mpande and Mpande's son Cetewayo. I need to know the political structure of each chieftain's regime, along with the customs and traditions. I want to know every facet of the nineteenth-century Zulus, including what they ate, drank and what kind of tribal society supported their existence.

"I need to know how they built their homes, their agriculture and the status of their women and children during each reign." Cal opened his eyes and stared at a smiling Lauren.

"Anything else, Cal?"

He returned her smile. "Yes, there is. The wars. I want to know who the Europeans were who challenged the Zulus for an empire that dominated southern Africa from the Zambezi River to Cape Colony. I need an accounting of any skirmish between the Zulus and the Europeans and a detailed description of a ferocious battle which rivals the battle of the Little Bighorn, where at Isandhlwana the British were nearly annihilated when they lost twelve hundred men on January 22, 1879. Another important battle resulted in a decisive British victory at Ulundi on July 4, 1879."

Lauren digested this information, knowing it would be months before she completed nearly one hundred years of Zulu history.

"How well do you know your Zulu chiefs?" she questioned.

"I know enough about them to write them as fully developed characters," he confessed. But at that moment Caleb Samuels wanted to know about Lauren Taylor. He wanted to know everything about her: what she liked, didn't like. What made her laugh, and what made her cry.

He wanted to know whether she was sentimental; whether she had a sense of humor; who was her favorite author? What kind of music did she enjoy? Whether she liked to dance or if she had been kissed—really kissed with the passion a man summoned deep within him; a passion he kept hidden until the right woman came into his life.

But was Lauren Taylor the right woman? He, Caleb Samuels who had met and known more women than he wanted to admit, wanted a little slip of a woman who was barely out of her teens. A woman whom he knew, instinctively, was all woman.

Cal caught a glimpse of Judith as she came out of the house. "It's time for breakfast," he informed Lauren.

Rising to his feet, he extended his hand to Lauren. He grasped her slender fingers, pulling her fluidly to her feet. He cradled her hand in the bend of his elbow and led her back to the house.

Walking beside her, holding her hand possessively, seemed so easy, so natural, as a slender thread of attraction bound them together.

Lauren shared the morning and afternoon with Cal, sharing meals and discussing the format of his book series. Cal's editor joined them after lunch, but the session was conducted with an undercurrent of tension; tension felt only by Lauren and Cal.

Cal waited for the other man to leave, then leaned across the small table and captured Lauren's hand, stopping her scrawling notes on a steno pad.

"Enough, Lauren," he ordered softly. "We've worked enough today. Remember, you owe me a dinner date. We both need to unwind."

She remembered Bob Ferguson's remark about the festive nightlife on Cay Verde, and while she had been on the island for two days she had not taken the opportunity to sample that festivity.

"That sounds wonderful."

Cal glanced down at his watch. "If it's all right with you we'll leave around eight."

Three hours later Lauren sat beside Cal in the vintage Mercedes, clutching the edge of her seat as the car sped over the unpaved back road. A warm breeze whipped her freshly shampooed curling hair around her face.

Swallowing painfully, she closed her eyes. "Cal . . . Caleb?"

"Yes, Lauren," he replied, not taking his gaze off the road.

Her heart pounded painfully in her chest. "Do you have to speed?"

Cal slowed the car. "Am I frightening you?"

"Just don't drive so fast," she insisted.

Cal smiled. The little girl in Lauren has surfaced. He covered her left hand with his right, holding it protectively on his hard thigh. "I'd never do anything to put you in danger," he crooned softly.

Lauren felt the flexing and unflexing of the muscles in Cal's thigh through the fabric of his slacks whenever he applied pressure to the gas or brake pedals. He had captured her fingers, not releasing them, and after a while she didn't want him to let her go. Sitting beside Caleb Samuels, having him hold her, offered her a sense of protection she had never felt with another man.

Cal parked outside a large structure that resembled a one-story thatched pagoda. Bright lights, live music and laughter spilled over and greeted them the moment the door opened.

Cal was greeted with a familiar fondness by many of the revelers, and for the first time Lauren felt the force of his celebrity status. He held her waist possessively when he introduced her to people Lauren had read about in *Town and Country* or *Vanity Fair*. When asked about the release of his next book Cal mumbled something inane, which seemed to satisfy most of the curious partygoers.

Cal asked the maître d' for a table in a secluded corner and within minutes he and Lauren were seated. They sampled a platter of fried sweet bananas, codfish fritters, a savory rice with pigeon peas and spicy shredded cabbage.

Lauren took a swallow of her rum punch, her large dark eyes fixed on Cal's smiling face. "I don't think I'll ever get used to one-hundred-fifty-proof rum. Everything I eat or drink has rum in it."

Cal's eyes swept slowly over her wind-tossed curling hair, then down to her full lush mouth. "You'll get used to it."

Feeling the potent effects of the punch, Lauren shook her head, the curls dancing provocatively over her forehead. "I don't think I want to get used to it."

Cal held out his hand. "Are you steady enough to dance with me?"

"If I'm not, you'll have to hold me up."

"That shouldn't be too difficult. I doubt if you weigh a hundred pounds."

"A hundred and three," she confirmed.

"You're some heavyweight, aren't you?" he teased, coming around the table and helping her stand.

Cal led her onto the dance area and into the slow steps of a throbbing tune with a distinctive reggae beat. This dance was the first of Lauren's many dances with Cal as he led her expertly from one rhythm to another as the live band played on tirelessly.

Lauren pleaded thirst and Cal ordered another round of drinks. They sat at the bar, swaying to the beat of taped music coming through massive speakers. Like Cal and Lauren, the band had also taken a break.

Leaning over, Cal pulled a damp curl away from Lauren's cheek, and without a warning his mouth replaced his fingers against her moist face.

"Thank you," he mumbled.

Her eyes widened in surprise as she stared into the depths of his amber gaze. The flickering flames from a small candle on the bar highlighted the gold in his eyes and in his skin.

"For what?" she questioned.

"For being here with me; for being you, and for being so beautiful, Lauren Taylor."

Everything disappeared around Lauren, except for the magnetic man beside her; she was aware of his warmth and strength, her own face growing warm under the heat of his gaze; their eyes locked as their chests rose and fell in unison.

His large hand took her face and held it gently, and even though Lauren wanted to, she couldn't pull away. His touch was hypnotic, spellbinding, and she leaned closer, wanting him to touch more than her face.

Lauren's forehead dropped to his shoulder as she tried bringing her fragile emotions under control. What was the matter with her? She hadn't known him—no she didn't know this man, so why was she reacting so recklessly toward him. Was it possible that she could feel an immediate and a total attraction for Caleb Samuels?

Gazes were turned in their direction and when Cal looked up he noted them. He was conscious of Lauren pressed against his chest, but more than that he was aware of his reputation, and the need to protect her surfaced without warning. Malicious gossip had followed him most of his adult life but he didn't want that gossip linked to Lauren.

Curving a strong arm around her tiny waist, he assisted her from the tall stool. "Let's go home, darling."

Lauren nodded, winding her arms inside his jacket and around his back.

The floral fragrance from Lauren's hair and body tested the limits of Cal's self-control as he escorted her outside into the sultry night air. He helped her into the car before taking his seat behind the wheel. A low rumble of thunder shook the night and he pressed a button for the convertible top. Fat drops of rain splattered the windshield within minutes.

Lauren closed her eyes, pressing her head against the leather seat, unaware of the speedometer inching above the island's legal speed limit.

She tried sorting out her feelings for Caleb Samuels and failed miserably, and she was dismayed at the magnitude of her own desire for him. She had known of the strong passion within her even though she had denied the passion over and over.

The speed of the car, the low rumbling of thunder, the flash and crack of lightning and the pounding of rain on the canvas top echoed the blood rushing throughout Lauren's system.

She wanted Caleb Samuels—his maddening arrogance, literary brilliance, gentle touch, caressing voice and his overwhelming virility.

Her heart was pumping uncontrollably when he stopped the car at the house and came around to help her out. Within seconds his linen jacket, slacks and cotton shirt were soaked from the torrential downpour. Gathering Lauren in his arms, Cal raced toward the house and Lauren felt the rain pelting her hair and soaking her white organdy halter top and skirt. The moisture, heat and scent from their bodies lingered sensuously in her nostrils.

Once inside the entry, Cal lowered Lauren to her feet. "I think I'm lost in the Bermuda Triangle," she slurred, referring to the rum-laced drink she had consumed.

Cal smiled down at the dreamy expression on her face. "You won't drown, darling. I'll make certain . . ."

Lauren was too relaxed to register Cal's endearment, but she did notice his startled look when he didn't complete his statement. She followed his gaze, looking down. Her wet top was plastered to her chest like skin, the dark circle of her nipples showing through the finely woven white fabric.

Cal moved toward her without moving. He kissed her with his eyes, his tenderness and repressed desire.

"Caleb," she whispered as his lips brushed against hers.

His mouth covered hers, demanding a response. Lauren returned the kiss, exhibiting a hunger that belied her outward calm.

Cal felt her hunger, answering it with a deprivation he hadn't known he possessed. Without warning and for the second time that night Lauren was a captive in Cal's arms, as he took the stairs two at a time, his mouth still fixed to hers.

Lauren pulled her mouth away, gasping for much-needed air and pressed her face to his chest. His heart pumped strongly under her cheek.

She knew what was to come, but was helpless to stop it. She didn't want to stop it. She wanted to give in to the delicious desire dissolving her into a mass of quivering, pulsating ecstasy.

Cal carried Lauren into her bedroom, shutting the door behind them with his foot. He set her down on her bed, walking back to lock the door and light a fat, scented candle on the floor by the door. The flickering flame threw long and short shadows on the ceiling and walls, yet the flame wasn't bright enough to highlight the bed where Lauren lay. The window shutters were open and the rain-swept wind flowed into the room, giving the space a freshly washed fragrance.

Lauren blinked in the muted darkness, but could not see beyond her hand. She heard the whisper of fabric as Cal shed his clothes.

Closing her eyes, she let her senses take over as she felt the side of the bed dip. She opened her eyes, jerking when his fingers went to the waistband of her skirt.

"I won't hurt you, baby. Trust me," he said softly.

Lauren nodded her assent and he undressed her, gasping audibly once he had bared her body to his gaze.

Settling himself over her trembling limbs, he kissed her mouth and Lauren felt her insides warming, melting. His tongue caressed her lower lip, then the upper, and she began groaning once he took full possession of her mouth.

The heat began with the kiss and spread to her breasts and still further down to her belly.

Cal's mouth traced the heat, from her lips to her breasts, ribs, belly, staking its claim to her core.

Lauren trembled and moaned under his rapacious tongue. Caleb Samuels was doing things to her she did not know existed. He made her feel things she had never felt before—not with any man, and she wanted him the way she had never wanted any man.

Moving up her body, Cal took her hand and guided to his thighs. "I want you, darling. But I have to know if you want me."

Her small hand closed around his flesh and she felt his heat, his fullness and his hardness.

"Love me, Caleb. Please," she moaned.

Cal positioned himself at the entrance to her femininity, pushing gently. Slowly, gently he entered her tight, hot flesh, clenching his teeth to keep from crying out his own pleasure.

She took him inch by inch, until he was fully sheathed in her moist body.

Cal began a slow, stroking motion, withdrawing and plunging deeply into her womb. Lauren began moving in concert with him, keeping his rhythm before setting one of her own.

He felt her hot breath on his neck, the bite of her fingernails on his buttocks and the soft whimpers rising from the back of her throat.

The pleasure began building, soaring and rushing until Cal and Lauren were rendered mindless by the raw act of possession.

Everything exploded at once. Their primal screams merged, the moment ecstasy shattered them into fiery tongues of fire.

They lay together, a tangle of limbs in the flickering candlelight, waiting for their breathing to resume its normal rate.

Lauren snuggled closer to Cal's body and soon there was only the sound of her soft breathing blending with the now softer patter of falling rain.

Cal shifted, pulling a sheet up over their moist bodies. He smiled in the darkness. He would never have guessed that innocent-looking Lauren Taylor was capable of such passion. More passion than any other woman had ever offered him.

Lauren awoke the next morning and found Cal staring at her. "Good morning," she said shyly.

Tucking a finger under her chin, he pressed a light kiss to her lips. "Good morning, darling."

Lowering her head, she kissed his shoulder, her left arm sliding over his flat belly as Cal buried his face in her hair.

Cal could not believe he had spent the entire night with Lauren beside him. He usually made love to a woman, but never slept with them. He wanted no ties, no claims, no declarations of love and no commitments.

He wondered whether he didn't sleep with them because he was afraid of commitment—afraid that his life would mirror his parents' turbulent marriages.

But why hadn't he left Lauren Taylor's bed? What was so different about her?

Wasn't it time for him to put his fears to rest? Could he hope to capture the love and security eluding him for years?

He had to find out if Lauren was the one to exorcise his ghosts. He turned to her, slowly and methodically preparing her to accept his passion, and after making love to her a second time he knew he loved Lauren with a love that was quiet, gentle and safe.

Lauren lay in bed on the fifth night of her stay on Cay Verde, her heart pounding wildly in her chest. "We don't have to get married," she protested.

"Yes, we do," Cal argued with a smile. "I will not sleep with you again unless we're married."

She bit down on her lower lip, frowning. She did not want to think of Cal not making love to her. Sharing her body with him opened up a world of passion she had not thought possible, and before she succumbed to the numbed sleep of a sated lover she prayed her time with him would never end.

Cal pulled her body over his, her legs nestled intimately between his. He kissed her tousled hair. "I love you, Lauren. I didn't think it would be possible for me to fall in love with you so quickly," he said incredulously, "but it happened."

What Cal didn't tell Lauren was that she was the first uncomplicated thing he had had in his life in a long time. He was tired of sleeping around, tired of making idle chitchat at social functions and he was tired of being alone despite a wide circle of acquaintances. Right at this moment, he realized he was ready to settle down and have children. He wanted Lauren to have his children, and for the first time since he began sleeping with a woman with whom he hadn't taken measures to prevent contraception.

Lauren rested her chin on her arms folded on Cal's chest. "Do you propose to every woman you sleep with?"

His golden eyes moved slowly over her face. "No. And I've never proposed to a woman before."

Lauren shifted her eyebrows. "I'm the first?"

He nodded, smiling. "You're the first."

She was filled with a strange inner excitement with the

knowledge that Cal loved her, because she believed she had fallen in love with him the first night she met him on the beach. He had overwhelmed her from the first time she shared his bed and he continued to overwhelm her, refusing to believe it was sex or his celebrity status.

"I'll be good to you, Lauren," he said, seeing her look of indecision. "I'll protect you, darling, and I'll always love you."

Lauren lowered her head, willing the tears behind her eyelids not to fall as his hands trailed over her back and hips.

"Please, darling," he pleaded.

"When do you want to marry?" she asked, her voice muffled in his neck.

"Tomorrow."

Her head came up quickly, revealing the tears staining her cheeks. "Why tomorrow? Why the rush?"

Cradling her face between his hands, Cal kissed the end of her nose. "I found you on Cay Verde and I want to make certain you belong to me before we leave Cay Verde." What he didn't tell her was that he was afraid of losing her.

"Caleb . . ."

"It's going to be all right, darling," he interrupted. "I'll make you happy."

Lauren floundered before the brilliance of his gaze, but not before she caught a glimpse of what Caleb Samuels had never exhibited to another human being—vulnerability.

You love him, her heart pounded rhythmically. At that moment she did love him—with all of her heart.

"Do you love me?" he asked.

"Yes," Lauren whispered, tears flowing unchecked down her face.

"Will you marry me?"

"Yes, Caleb."

* * *

The following afternoon found Lauren Vernice Taylor exchanging vows with Caleb Baldwin Samuels II in a private ceremony in a tiny white church with only the local island minister and his wife present.

Cal slipped the signet ring off his little finger and placed it on the ring finger of Lauren's left hand, kissing her passionately. They accepted the good wishes of the minister and his wife who showered them with a hail of rice.

He led her back to the car, leaning down to brush his lips over hers. "I'll buy you a ring when we return to Boston. Speaking of Boston," he continued excitedly, "we'll stay with my grandfather until we decide where we want to live."

Lauren stared up at the stranger she had just married. "Your grandfather?"

"He practically raised me," Cal informed her. "He's wonderful, darling. I carry his name."

Her brow furrowed in concentration. "Don't tell me your grandfather is the same Dr. Samuels who won the Nobel Prize for Medicine for his work in identifying gene abnormalities in fetuses?"

"He's the same," he admitted proudly.

She felt her first pang of doubt when she realized she had been a little too hasty in agreeing to marry a man she had known less than a week. She knew nothing about him or his family.

However, she pushed the thread of doubt to the farthest recesses of her mind when she lay in bed with Cal on their wedding night. Their lovemaking signaled a change in their lives. Being married had added a special quality to their coming together.

Cradled in Cal's arms and luxuriating in the aftermath of their passion Lauren knew she was in love with her husband.

But the fairy tale had ended when they returned to

Boston. Lauren walked out on Cal and when she returned to Summit Publishing she asked to be relieved from her assignment. Bob Ferguson did not ask her why, but he had received word that Caleb Samuels decided not to write the series, saying personal business dictated he return to Barcelona.

Bob suspected all had not gone well between his researcher and C. B. Samuels, so he waited for Lauren to confide in him.

Three months later Lauren handed him her resignation, and he knew he would never uncover what had occurred on Cay Verde.

Chapter Four

Drew Taylor-Samuels lay on crisp clean sheets decorated with characters from a popular animated science-fiction series, smiling up at his mother. "I want a story about the space invaders."

Lauren sat on a rocker beside her son's bed. This was a story-telling session that would not include Jamal, Space Warriors or Dr. Seuss. The story she planned to tell Drew was real even though it hadn't been written.

"I want to tell you about Caleb Samuels."

A frown formed between Drew's golden-brown eyes. "Who's that?"

"Caleb Samuels is your father," Lauren replied.

Drew's eyes widened as his mouth dropped slightly. "My daddy?"

Lauren nodded. "Yes, your daddy."

The young boy sat up, grinning. "I like stories about my daddy."

Lauren exhaled audibly, closing her eyes briefly. "This isn't a story, Drew," she began slowly. "What I'm trying to say is that your father is here."

"Here?" Drew leaned forward, pulling back the colorful sheets.

"No, darling, he's not here now." Vertical slashes marred the child's forehead. "He wants to see you."

The frown vanished quickly. "When, Mommy?"

"He's coming here to see you tomorrow."

"Where is he now?"

"In Boston."

"With grandma and grandpa?"

"No, Drew. He lives in his own house."

Drew pushed out his lower lip. "I thought you said he had a house in Spain."

"He does, but he's in the United States now."

"Is he going to stay in the United States?"

That was a question which Lauren couldn't answer and refused to try to answer. "I don't know, Drew," she said instead.

"When I see my daddy I'll ask him," Drew replied, puffing up his narrow chest. He stared at his mother, not seeing the tension tightening her facial muscles. "That was a good story, Mommy."

Lauren managed a tight smile. "Yes, Drew. Yes it was." Rising from the rocker, she kissed her son's forehead. "Don't forget to say your prayers before you go to sleep."

Drew lay down, closing his eyes and smiling. "I won't forget."

She turned off the bedside lamp and made her way out of Drew's bedroom to her bedroom where she fell weakly onto her bed. She had done it—told Drew his father's name, told him Cal was coming to meet him, and now all she had to do was wait.

The incessant ringing shattered the vestiges of Cal's sound sleep. Reaching for the telephone, he knocked it over. Mumbling a curse under his breath, he hung over the side of the bed, his fingers searching for the annoying instrument.

"Caleb?" came a husky female voice through the receiver.

"Yeah?"

"It's Lauren."

He sat up, all traces of sleep vanishing. "Yes, Lauren?"

"Drew wants to meet you."

Cal barely registered her words. His heart rate increased, pumping his blood, hot and wild, throughout his body.

"When?" Resting his head against the bed's headboard, he squeezed his eyes tightly. He had not met the boy, and already he was falling apart.

"If you can be here by eleven-thirty, we'll share lunch together."

"Give me the directions," Cal demanded. He listened intently, scribbling furiously on the pad on the bedside table. He repeated them into the receiver.

"I'll see you later," Lauren said quietly, then the line went dead.

Cal held the receiver to his ear, listening to the dial tone. He returned the receiver to its cradle and picked up his watch. North Grafton was about forty miles west of Boston and he had a little more than an hour to get there. Throwing the sheet off his naked body, he headed for the bathroom.

Shaving became a game of chance when his shaking hand cut the tender skin over his throat, not once but twice. He splashed cold water onto his face, then sucked in deep drafts of air. He had to slow down or he would never live to meet his son.

Cal straightened, looking at his reflection staring back at him in the mirror over the basin. "My son," he whispered to the reflection. "I have a son."

By some minor miracle Cal showered, dressed and managed not to wreck his car during his high-speed drive from Boston to North Grafton.

The countryside was awash with color with the advent of summer in all of its glory. Trees, lawns and shrubs were resplendent in their verdant, lush dress. Cal caught sight of the small convenience store Lauren had mentioned, and turned down the narrow road leading to her house.

Downshifting, he slowed as a tiny furred creature scurried across the road, disappearing into the nearby woods.

Lauren had chosen well. Towering trees shading homes, light vehicular traffic and spacious lawns made North Grafton an ideal place to raise a child, and Cal was far enough from the noise and pollution of Boston to appreciate the town's sleepy quaintness and charm.

He spied Lauren's dark blue sedan and maneuvered into the driveway behind it. The screen door to the large white farmhouse opened and Lauren walked out. She rested a slender hip against the porch column, staring down at him.

Cal swallowed painfully as he unfolded his long legs from the low-slung sports car. Gone were the silk dress, sheer hose and heels. In their place were a pair of well-worn jeans, a T-shirt and bare feet. With her bare feet and unmade face Lauren looked more like seventeen than twenty-seven. She looked as young as she had when he first met her. Her eyes narrowed, her gaze going to the small white plastic bag he held in his left hand.

"I picked up a little something for Drew," he explained, walking up the steps. He stopped two steps below her and met her level gaze.

Lauren gave him a warm smile and Cal couldn't help but return it. "Thank you, Cal. Drew always gets excited when someone buys him something."

I'm not just someone, Cal thought. He was the boy's father. He peered over her head at the door. "I . . . I'd like to see him please."

Lauren turned, missing the anxiety thinning Cal's mouth. "Of course." She opened the door, waiting for Cal to precede her into the house.

Cal walked into a spacious living room, seeing only the young boy seated on a sofa in a colorful country French

design. Ribbons of sunlight seeping through the lace cur-
tains at the many windows confirmed that the child was
truly an issue of his loins. Just looking at the boy was
enough. Drew Michael Taylor-Samuels *was* his son.

They shared the same lean face, high cheekbones and
forehead, eyes, lean jaw and dimpled chin. Cal moved
closer, smiling. Drew also had a tiny mole near the left eye
that gave his young face a distinctive quality. He was so
filled with emotion that he wanted to shout out his joy, but
decided not to startle or frighten the child.

Lauren sat down beside Drew, cradling him to her
breasts. "Drew, this is your father," she explained softly.
She watched Drew staring up at the tall man who looked
so much like him. "He's waited a long time to meet you."
Glancing up at Cal, she said, "Cal, this is Drew."

Cal hunkered down in front of Drew, extending his
right hand. "I'm pleased to meet you." His eyes were
shining like polished citrines.

Drew crossed and uncrossed his sneakered feet, staring
down at the scuffed toes, his hands sandwiched between
his jean-covered knees. Slowly, reluctantly he extended
his right hand. "Hi."

Lauren released Drew, nodded at Cal, then walked out
of the living room.

Cal sat down next to Drew, smiling. The child was
perfect. "How are you?" he asked, not knowing what else
to say to a child.

Drew would not look at Cal. "Good. Mommy said you
lived far away in Spain and that you don't know me."

Cal caught Drew's chin and raised his face. "That's
true, Drew. If I had known that I had a son I would've
come back a long time ago to find you."

Drew's amber-colored eyes widened. "Really?"

Cal shifted his arching eyebrows. "Really."

Bright color flushed Drew's sun-browned tawny
cheeks. "Do you have another boy?"

Cal's laugh was full and rich when he threw back his

head. "No," he finally answered. "You're my only child."
He extended his hand with the small plastic shopping bag.
"I didn't know what to bring you, but I hope you'll like
this."

Drew gave him a tentative glance before reaching for
the bag. Cal knew immediately that he had chosen well.

"Wow! Oh, wow," Drew exclaimed breathlessly. He
slipped the dark blue baseball cap, emblazoned with a red
B, on his head. "Thank you," he got out in a shy voice,
offering Cal a hint of a smile.

The tightness in Cal's chest eased. He dropped an arm
around Drew's shoulders, then suddenly without warning
the child was in his arms as he cradled his son to his chest.

Pressing his lips to Drew's soft, curling black hair, Cal
closed his eyes. "I'll never leave you." His composure
faltered when Drew wound his arms around his neck,
holding him tightly. "No matter what happens between
me and your mother I'll never leave you," he whispered
against his son's ear.

"I don't want you to go away, Daddy."

Cal experienced a riot of emotions. He didn't know
whether to laugh or cry. Drew had called him "Daddy."

Burying his face against Drew's neck, Cal did not see
Lauren reenter the living room and observe them. She bit
down hard on her lower lip and slipped quietly to the
kitchen.

Tears Lauren had not permitted to fall years before fell
now. She had always prided herself on being strong, facing adversity head-on. But this time she could not help the
soft sobs draining her as she buried her face in her hands
and released the guilt she had carried for so long that it
had become a part of her everyday existence.

She had made a mistake not telling Cal about her
pregnancy, and only now could she admit that to herself.

She had cheated Cal; she had cheated Drew, and she
had cheated herself out of the love the three of them
could've shared.

She made it to the half-bath off the kitchen and bathed her swollen eyes with cold water. She dried her face, reliving the scene with Cal holding Drew. Man and child; father and son; they had found each other.

The realization of what had happened pierced her like a knife. Drew had found his father and Cal his son. But where would that leave her?

Cal said he wouldn't fight her for Drew, but his claim did not have to be physical. Just by virtue of being who he was, a male figure to a male child, would that be enough for Drew to switch loyalties?

She had not had to share Drew with anyone for almost four years. He was hers and hers alone. Even her mother complained that she had become too possessive with the child. But Cal had as much a right to his son as she. Lauren wondered if she would be selfless enough to give up a little of Drew to his father.

She left the bathroom and returned to the kitchen, turning on a burner under a large pot of water, then busied herself setting the table in a dining nook. She added spaghetti to the boiling water and heated a casserole dish filled with a fragrant marinara sauce and meatballs in the microwave oven.

Drew pulled Cal into the kitchen. "You can wash up in here, Daddy. Mommy gets really, really mad if I don't wash my hands when it's time to eat," he whispered softly.

Cal's brilliant gaze impaled Lauren as he stared at her, visually examining her face. He knew she had been crying.

"Mommy is very special, Drew," he said almost reverently. "And we must always make certain she's happy."

Drew steered Cal toward the small bathroom. "Mommy's always happy. She laughs and sings all the time."

Cal glanced back over his shoulder at Lauren. A slight smile crinkled her puffy eyes. "That's good to know."

Drew and Cal made a big show of washing their hands.

Drew squealed when Cal flicked the water off his hands and it sprayed his face.

Drew put his hands under the running water and shook them out wildly.

"I give up," Cal pleaded. He glanced up at the mirror over the basin, pointing. Droplets of water dotted the glass.

"Uh-oh," they both chorused, then dissolved into a paroxysm of giggles.

Cal tore a sheet of paper toweling from a rack. "I think we'd better clean this up," he whispered conspiratorially.

Drew was still giggling when he slipped into his place on the bench at the table. "Sit next to me, Daddy."

Cal complied obediently, watching Lauren fill a glass at Drew's place setting with milk. He had spent a restless night trying to sort out his feelings after seeing her again, shaken because he realized he still loved her and loved her with the same intensity he had felt on Cay Verde.

After her betrayal, after her deceit, he had continued to love her.

He was amazed that after five years he had changed, yet his feelings for Lauren hadn't changed. Five years before he had been twenty-eight—a very jaded twenty-eight, and Lauren had not been wrong when she told him he was too old for her. By that time he had lived on two continents, socialized with a hedonistic group and had written four best sellers.

He had blamed his behavior and lifestyle on his being the offspring of a tempestuous relationship between a dancer and a noted Boston entertainment attorney who married, divorced, remarried only to divorce a second and final time.

Cal had also spent half of his childhood crossing the Atlantic Ocean between Boston and Barcelona, and when he met Lauren Taylor she offered him what he had sought for a long time—peace, a respite.

Lauren sat down, bowing her head. Drew did the same.

Cal lowered his head, feeling somewhat sheepish that it had been a long time, too long, since he had offered thanks for the food placed before him.

"Will you please say grace, Cal?" Lauren asked in a quiet voice.

Cal racked his memory, coming up with one he had learned as a child in Barcelona. The words flowed, fluidly and musically. Both Lauren and Drew raised their head, staring at him.

Lauren blinked slowly, studying his smiling face. "Don't you know one in English?"

He shifted his eyebrows, the gesture reminding her of Drew's. "No."

Drew gave his father a sidelong glance. "What did you say?"

Cal stared down at Drew. "It's Spanish. I thanked God for the food, the hands that prepared it . . ."

"That's Mommy," Drew interrupted.

Cal glanced over at Lauren. "Yes, that's Mommy. And I also thanked the farmers who grew the food."

Drew puffed up his narrow chest. "Say some more Spanish, Daddy."

Cal ruffled Drew's hair. "Would you like to learn to speak Spanish?"

"Oh yes! Yes, yes, yes!" Drew squealed.

Cal smiled at his animated expression. "We'll begin tomorrow. If that's all right with your mother," he added, noting a slight frown from Lauren.

"Can we, Mommy?"

Her frown vanished as quickly as it had formed. "It's 'may we,' Drew." Her large dark eyes shifted to Cal. "Maybe you should go slowly. Not too much too soon."

Cal knew exactly what she meant, and his mouth tightened. Lauren wasn't going to let him back in her life.

* * *

Lauren was quiet during the meal, electing to let Cal and Drew interact with each other. It wasn't easy, but she had to let them have their time together.

Cal and Drew reached for the last slice of crisp Italian bread at the same time. "Let's choose for it, Daddy."

"Two out of three gets it," Cal announced.

"Odds, even, odds," Drew shrieked. "I win!"

Cal turned down his mouth, pouting, and Lauren couldn't stop her laughter from bubbling up and out. He glared at her.

"What's so funny?"

Lauren smothered her laughter. "You. I thought you were going to cry."

Drew broke the slice in half. "Here, Daddy. I don't want you to cry."

A high-pitched yelp and barking filtered through the open windows and Lauren stared across the table at Drew. It was what they had been expecting for days.

"Missy's having her puppies," Drew whispered, his eyes wide and glittering with excitement and anticipation.

Lauren slid off the bench, stopping to slip her bare feet into a pair of worn espadrilles. Drew urged Cal off the bench and followed his mother to the garage.

"Don't get too close," Lauren warned Drew as he and Cal joined her in the coolness of the garage. A large Old English sheepdog lay on a pile of blankets in a corner.

Cal moved closer and hunkered down, laying a hand on the bitch's head. Missy's dark eyes opened and closed as she labored to bring forth the life writhing within her distended abdomen.

"Don't touch her, Daddy!" Drew shouted. "She bites."

Cal went to his knees and pressed his ear against Missy's heaving side. "This little lady's in too much pain to bite. All she wants is to have her babies and rest."

Lauren and Drew could not believe that Missy hadn't snapped at or bitten Cal. They had found the abandoned dog two weeks after moving into the large farmhouse.

Lauren had not been ready to assume the responsibility of caring for a dog when she had to care for a preschooler and make her home habitable for the coming winter. Somehow she managed to get close enough to the snarling animal to wash away the dirt and grime to see the abject abuse the dog had endured. The deep, raw gashes under the thick coat of black-and-white fur sickened her.

She pushed the dog into the back of her car and drove like someone possessed to Tufts University School of Veterinarian Medicine. Missy underwent surgery and spent three days at the school recovering from the surgery and her infected wounds. Lauren was handed a bill and the news that Missy was pregnant.

Not only had she been saddled with a house that needed numerous minor repairs, but also a pregnant dog who snapped and growled at anyone who came within five feet of her.

"How's she doing, Daddy?"

Cal continued stroking Missy's side. "She's doing just fine."

Lauren went to her knees beside Cal. "I can't believe she likes you," she said in awe. "I feed her, but that doesn't stop her from trying to bite me."

"An animal can sense your fear or anxiety," Cal replied. "Missy knows I'm not going to hurt her."

"Somebody hurt Missy real bad before Mommy and I found her," Drew stated proudly.

Cal extended a hand to Drew. "Come pet her."

Drew took a few steps backwards, shaking his head. "Oh no. She'll bite me."

Cal glanced up, noting Drew's anguished expression. "Try it, Drew. She won't bite you."

"Don't force him, Cal," Lauren said, recognizing Drew's reluctance and fear.

Cal looked at Lauren, seeing her tender expression as she stared at Drew. "How's he to overcome his fear if he doesn't face it, darling?"

Lauren did not visibly react to the endearment that seemed to slip fluidly from Cal. Her gaze narrowed. "He's only three, Caleb."

"And he's old enough to have a pet he's not afraid of, Lauren. What's the use of having the dog around if neither of you are going to interact with it," he countered.

"Missy is a watchdog," Lauren shot back.

Cal grunted under his breath. "Some damn watchdog," he mumbled low enough so that Drew couldn't hear him. "Not only does she frighten the neighbors, but also her master."

Lauren stared at the attractive cleft in his strong chin, then pulled her gaze back to his luminous eyes. "Mind your own business, Caleb Samuels," she replied softly.

He flashed a maddening grin. "It's too late, Lauren Samuels. Drew's my business. And you're also my business."

Lauren felt a shock of annoyance. He had continued to refer to her as a Samuels. "Wrong. And stop calling me Lauren Samuels."

Cal leaned closer. "I didn't give you up, Lauren. You walked out on me because you were a coward, and I don't acknowledge the actions of a coward." She opened her mouth to defend herself, but he stopped her, stating, "We'll talk about it later."

Her jaw snapped loudly and she gritted her teeth. Lauren knew she was not going to have it easy with Caleb Samuels. She had only spent a week with him—a glorious week, but Drew had permitted her a glimpse of what it would be like to live with the man. Not only had he inherited his father's looks but also his stubbornness. Lauren realized stubbornness flawed her own personality, but to recognize and meet it head-on in someone else was exasperating.

It was nearly an hour before Missy whelped her first puppy. Cal sat on the concrete floor, cradling Drew on his lap as the boy stroked the silky fur on Missy's massive head.

"She likes me," Drew replied in an awed tone. It was difficult for him to contain his excitement as he witnessed the miracle of birth when Missy birthed her second puppy.

There was complete silence as instinct took over. Missy took care of the membrane covering the minute, shivering puppies, cleaning them with her large pink tongue.

Lauren felt the tightness in her own chest ease as Missy nudged her tiny wet babies under her belly. The puppies managed, after several attempts, to locate the swollen nipples to begin nursing.

"Why don't they open their eyes, Daddy?"

Cal rested his chin on the top of Drew's head. "All babies are born with their eyes closed."

Drew glanced up at his father. "Even me?"

Cal glared at Lauren, his eyes saying what she knew his lips wouldn't. "Yes, Drew. Even you," he finally said.

Drew pointed at the nursing puppies. "Did you do that to me, Mommy?"

The heat in Lauren's face had nothing to do with the warmth of the summer afternoon as she watched Cal's gaze move to her breasts.

"Did you, Mommy?" Drew asked, repeating his question.

"Did you, Lauren?" Cal echoed with a sinister grin.

"Yes, I did," she replied, lifting her chin. "It's nature's way of feeding a baby," she explained to Drew.

Cal gave Lauren a nod and an approving smile. "I'm sorry I missed that experience, darling."

For a long moment Lauren stared at him. He was serious. Cal had missed so much and so had she. She had missed not sharing the news of her pregnancy with him, missed his watching her belly swell with his child, missed his soothing away her fears in the labor room, and she'd missed his expression when he could have witnessed the birth of his son; a son who was completely and undeniably his son—their son.

Cal eased Drew off his lap, rising to his feet. His tan slacks were streaked with dirt. Lauren noticed the dark smudges on his knees.

"Jeans are the norm when hanging out around here," she stated.

Cal glanced down at his slacks. "I'll remember that next time."

Drew had not moved from his kneeling position beside Missy. All of his attention was directed on the nursing puppies. "Can I stay and watch, Mommy?"

"Yes. But don't touch the puppies," she warned.

"I won't," Drew complied, not turning away from the whelping corner.

Lauren turned and went back into the house. She washed her hands, then began clearing the table of their half-eaten lunch.

Turning, she bumped into Cal. He took the plates from her hands. "I'll help you."

"No!" she shouted before she could stop herself.

"What's the matter?" There was an expression of genuine concern on his face.

"Just go, Caleb."

His jaw hardened. "Why?"

"I don't want your help."

"What do you want, Lauren?"

"I want you to leave *me* alone. You wanted to see your son and I've agreed to that, but that's where it ends. I don't want to have anything to do with you."

"I, I, I! That's all I hear from you, Lauren. It's always you and no one else. How about me, Lauren? How about Drew? What about Drew inheriting what is rightfully his?"

Lauren's temper flared, matching Cal's. "Let's clear the air about your grandfather's will. I do not and will not concede to his antiquated scheme of forcing us to stay together. This is not the Middle Ages."

Cal tried bringing his turbulent emotions under control. Losing his temper only fueled Lauren's. "He didn't put us together five years ago, Lauren. We married because we loved each other, not because anyone forced us to live together."

"That doesn't change the fact that a dead man is manipulating our lives."

"But he left us a way out."

Her gaze narrowed. "How's that?"

"We only have to remain married for a year, Lauren. That's only three hundred sixty-three more days than we had five years ago."

"But we have to live together."

"People who are married generally do live together."

"No, Cal," she replied, shaking her head for emphasis. "I can't."

He took a step closer, his breath washing over her face. "My grandfather let you off a lot easier than I would've done if I had discovered you had my child and not told me. In other words, he saved your butt, Lauren."

"What are you talking about?"

Cal prayed he would not explode. He still loved Lauren, still loved her passionately yet she would not let him come to her with love.

"I would've sued you for joint custody of my son." His eyes were cold, forbidding. "You were my wife when Drew was conceived, and as your husband I had a right to know that you were carrying my baby. No court of law would've denied me *that* right, Mrs. Samuels, while you willfully and deliberately kept me ignorant of that fact."

Lauren felt her composure break. "Then do it, Caleb! If you want revenge that badly—then sue me!" Her hands curled into tight fists.

"It's not about revenge, Lauren. It's about Drew and his future."

Lauren had thought about the money Dr. Samuels had bequeathed his great-grandson. She knew Drew probably would not need the money because she was certain Cal would provide for the child's future, but the fact remained that she wasn't given a choice in whether she wanted to be with Cal. The decision was taken out of her hands—their hands.

There was a pulse beat of silence before she asked, "If it's not revenge, then is it about not wanting Jacqueline to have the money?"

The tense lines around his mouth relaxed. "It's about not wanting Jacqueline to have the money," he admitted quietly. "But it's also about my son."

Lauren turned away from Cal, trying to sort out all that had happened in the past twenty-four hours. Why was it every time she encountered Caleb Samuels her life whirled out of orbit. What was there about him that unbalanced her?

"Please go," she ordered.

Cal stared at her straight back. "I'll leave, but I'll be back at six. We'll eat dinner out."

She bristled at his unexpected demand. "I . . ."

"Just be ready, Lauren," he snapped, turning on his heel and walking out of the kitchen and back to the garage, leaving Lauren glaring at his retreating figure.

Lauren evoked rage in him that stripped him of every shred of control he had over himself or his emotions. She had pushed and challenged him to new limits. She had unwittingly seduced him, married him, then walked out of his life, leaving a void that still lingered, and she had kept his son from him. But all of the deceit would end. This time Lauren would not be the only winner.

Chapter Five

Drew propped an elbow up on the table, supporting his chin on the heel of his right hand. "I thought we were going to McDonald's," he grumbled under his breath.

"Take your elbow off the table, Drew," Lauren chastised softly.

Cal laid aside the menu he had been reading. "What is it you want?" he asked the pouting child.

"A hamburger," Drew mumbled.

Cal smiled, placing a hand on his son's head. "I'm certain the chef can grind a sirloin steak into a burger."

Drew dropped his arm, the vertical slashes between his eyes vanishing quickly. "Can he make it fast?"

Cal glanced over at Lauren, noting the smile softening her moist, lush mouth. He arched a questioning brow and lifted broad shoulders under his cream-colored linen jacket.

Lauren leaned closer to Cal. "Drew wants to eat fast food so that he can get back home to the puppies," she explained.

"Yeah! The puppies," Drew shrieked.

Cal was at a loss for words. How could he explain to a three-year-old that he had to pull strings to garner a reservation at one of Boston's most elegant and popular restaurants to celebrate his newly discovered fatherhood?

Lauren came to his rescue, explaining, "The puppies

are like new babies, Drew. They'll sleep most of the time. The only thing they're going to do for the next week is eat and sleep."

Drew looked distressed. "When can they play with me?"

"Give them a couple of months."

The child did not look convinced as he looked at his mother under lowered lids. "How long is a couple of months?"

"Sixty days," Cal answered, his gaze fixed on Lauren's face, burning her with its brilliant intensity.

"I can count to a hundred and I know sixty is a lot," Drew said, frowning again.

"Sixty days will come very quickly, Drew," Lauren remarked, staring back at Cal.

"Too quickly," Cal retorted.

Sixty days was not a lot to Lauren. She couldn't wait for it to come because ever since she walked into the law offices of Barlow, Mann and Evans her life and her future was no longer her own to plan or control, because for the second time in her life she had lost control of herself. Why, she thought, was it always because of Caleb Samuels?

When she thought about it, her situation was more like something from a script for a TV soap than real life. How could Dr. Caleb B. Samuels being of sound mind and body formulate such a preposterous scheme? But had John Evans said that Dr. Samuels was of sound mind and body when he wrote his will?

She remembered the attorney stating that it was a simple will, then she ignored the rest of the legal language until he mentioned the equal distribution of the late doctor's estate.

"Mommy, there's Uncle Andy," Drew said in a hushed voice, temporarily forgetting about the puppies.

Turning, Lauren glanced over her shoulder. Andrew Monroe was heading for their table, grinning broadly.

Andrew's friendly smile did not falter when he recognized the man sitting between Lauren and Drew. Cal rose slightly and pulled back Lauren's chair as she stood up.

Lauren extended both hands, returning Andrew's appealing smile. "Who are you entertaining tonight?"

Andrew caught her fingers and pressed a light kiss to her lips. "Tonight I'm wining and dining."

Lauren cocked her head at an angle. "Who is she?"

Andrew's dark green eyes sparkled. "I don't know. She's a blind date."

Lauren looped her arm through the expensive fabric covering her agent's arm. "Andrew, I'd like you to meet Caleb Samuels." Cal was slow in rising to his feet. "Cal, Andrew Monroe, my agent." She felt the muscles bunch up under her hand and extracted her arm from Andrew's.

The two men gave each other predatory glares, then shook hands. Lauren let out her breath, unaware that she had been holding it in. The tension eased when Andrew hunkered down beside Drew's chair and dropped an arm around the boy's shoulders.

"What have you been up to, Drew?" Andrew asked.

"I have a daddy and Missy got new puppies," Drew managed to explain in one breath.

Andrew affected an expression of surprise. "Now, that's what I call headline news." He managed a smile for Cal. "You know you promised me a puppy, Champ."

Drew nodded. "Yup. But you can't have it for sixty days."

"I'll wait." Andrew stood, nodding at Cal. "My pleasure, Caleb." He winked at Lauren, leaning over and kissing her cheek. "I'll call you tomorrow," he told her quietly.

Cal seated Lauren before retaking his own place. He studied the menu without seeing the printed words. It was obvious Lauren and Andrew Monroe shared more than an agent-client relationship, and he did not have to have the intelligence quotient of a rocket scientist to know that Drew had been named for Andrew.

He stared at Andrew seated at a nearby table. Andrew's thick waving blond hair, electric green eyes and deep tropical tan made him a very attractive man; a man Cal was certain Lauren found attractive.

The sommelier's presence redirected Cal's attention. The man uncorked a bottle of wine and filled two glasses with the pale rosé Lauren had selected earlier to accompany their meal. Drew's glass was filled with a mixture of ginger ale and cherry syrup.

Cal's gaze caught and held Lauren's as she stared at him across the table. The light from the small lamp on the table reflected off her satiny dark skin. The scene was so natural yet so unnatural. They appeared the normal family dining out at the end of the week. But they were not a normal family. They were a family of strangers.

He raised his glass, smiling. "May I make the toast?"

"Please," Lauren conceded, raising her glass.

Drew, watching his parents, did the same.

The harder Cal tried to ignore the truth the more it persisted when he realized he had been waiting and holding out for Lauren. No woman he had ever met could duplicate or replace her. Knowing this he said solemnly, "A toast to the weddings, births, graduations and our grandchildren as we pass through this life together as a family."

It was another ten seconds before Lauren reacted to the toast. He had deceived her; he wanted more than a year of her life; he wanted a lifetime.

Her hand was steady, her voice low and controlled as she made her own toast. "To Caleb and Drew and a lifetime of love between father and son."

"Now me," Drew said, not wanting to be left out. "To my Mommy and Daddy and Missy and her puppies."

Lauren laughed, dispelling the strained mood created by Andrew's appearance and Cal's toast.

While dining, she caught a glimpse of Andrew's blind date, a young woman with curling red-gold hair. The angle of Andrew's head indicated he was quite enthralled with her.

Cal saw the direction of Lauren's gaze. "How long has Andrew been your agent?"

Lauren gave him a demure smile. "About four years."

Lowering his chin, Cal's lips twisted into a cynical smile. "You met him before you *met* me?"

"No. I met him after I'd met you. He became my agent and a good friend. I named Drew for him."

Cal put down his fork, placing both hands, palms down, on the pale pink tablecloth. The muscle in his jaw throbbed as he compressed his lips. "I take it you're close friends?"

Lauren heard the censure in his voice. "Very close." Her eyes met his, not wavering. "And we'll continue to be," she added quietly.

Cal blinked once. "I see."

She raised her chin. "Do you, Caleb?"

He refused to answer because what he wanted to say was better left unsaid. Andrew Monroe was not Drew's father yet he had secured a place of importance not only in his life, but also in Lauren's.

However, he could not blame Andrew if he was attracted to Lauren. There was something about her Cal had not been able to resist when he first met her. She was captivating. Whether she was stylishly dressed, as she was now in a polished cotton pumpkin-orange slip dress and matching collarless cropped jacket, or in a pair of jeans, Lauren Taylor-Samuels was alluring and incredibly feminine.

The soft light from the lamp shimmered on her smooth velvet-brown face, highlighting the darkness of her eyes, the delicate sweep of her high cheekbones and the sensual curve of her full, sexy mouth.

Her mouth. It fascinated him. The sweet fullness of her

lower lip he had tasted over and over until he was more intoxicated by the pliant flesh than the potent drinks he had consumed on Cay Verde.

Her voice. Even the sound of her voice, low and husky, had turned him on. He had lain in bed, eyes closed, listening to the sound of it as it filtered over his naked flesh like a luxurious fur pelt.

Bits and pieces of the days and nights he had made love to Lauren floated about him like the silent whisper of a snowflake. He could see it, feel it, but then it disappeared in the heat, leaving only a damp trace of its existence.

There had been times when he thought he had imagined her. She was in his life, and then she was gone.

Drew was nodding over his plate before he finished his hamburger and Cal signaled for the waiter and the check. Drew had forgone his regularly scheduled afternoon nap with the appearance of his father and the birth of the puppies.

Cal carried Drew out to the parking lot, placing him on the back seat of the car.

Lauren caught Cal's arm as he held the passenger door open for her. "No speeding, Caleb."

He frowned at her. "I wasn't speeding."

"Yes, you were," she argued.

"I was only doing seventy," he retorted.

"Then you were speeding."

Cal dangled a set of keys under her nose. "Do you want to drive?"

She took the keys from his fingers. Her heels rapped sharply on the asphalt as she walked around the car and slipped behind the wheel. She started up the engine, waiting for Cal to get into the car.

Leaning over, she stared up at him. "Are you getting in?"

Cal folded his long frame into her small car. "I didn't expect you to take me up on the offer."

"One thing you'll learn about me, Caleb Samuels, and

that is I accept all dares. Buckle your seat belt," she ordered when he crossed his arms over his chest.

His chuckle was low and confident. "I dare you to marry me again," he said quickly.

Her fingers tightened on the gearshift. "Marriage is excluded."

"Don't try to weasel out of it, Lauren."

"I'm not trying to weasel out of anything, Caleb."

"You're angry because you're caught in your own trap," he taunted.

Lauren shifted into first and maneuvered out of the parking space. "No, I'm not."

"Not trying to weasel out of your dare, or you're not angry?"

She concentrated on her driving. "The answer is no to both questions."

"Then why did you call me Caleb?"

"It's your name, isn't it?"

He arched his eyebrows, smiling. "Yes. But you only call me Caleb when you're angry or whenever we made love." He ignored her withering glare. "I used to love the little sounds you made in bed, Lauren."

Lauren stopped for a red light, catching a glimpse of his straight white teeth out of the corner of her eye.

"You're a pig."

"Why? Because I'm honest, darling."

"And I'm not?"

"No!" All traces of his teasing vanished quickly. "I'm going to ask you one question," he stated in a gentler tone, "and I want you to give me an honest answer. If you can't or won't, then don't say anything. But please, please, Lauren, don't lie to me again."

Lauren was angry; angry with herself and that she had permitted Cal to bait her. She did not have to look at him to feel his tension. She felt it radiating all around her.

"What is it you want to know?"

"Why did you leave me?"

Lauren stared out through the windshield. She was stiff; stiff and brittle enough to shatter into a million pieces if he touched her, and she could not look at Cal or she would lose control.

"I was afraid," she whispered.

Cal moved as close as his seat belt would permit him. "You were what?"

Lauren blinked back tears. "I . . . I was so afraid, Caleb."

"Pull over and stop," Cal ordered. Lauren signaled, maneuvered out of traffic and parked. "I'll drive," he informed her when he noted her deathlike grip on the steering wheel.

Lauren pressed her head back against the headrest, trying valiantly to bring her emotions under control. Unbuckling her seat belt, she slipped out of the car, exchanging seats with Cal.

Cal started the car, savagely shifting into gears. The sound of Lauren's voice telling him that she had been afraid unnerved and angered him.

He had wasted almost five years—*they* had wasted five years. If he had insisted that she give him a reason other than the one she had they would not have lost those years.

There was complete silence on the return drive to North Grafton, neither Lauren nor Cal initiating conversation.

Cal pulled into the driveway, turning off the engine. "I'll carry Drew," he said, and Lauren nodded.

She unlocked the front door and led the way through the living room and up the stairs to the second floor. Flipping on a wall switch, Lauren looked down before stepping into Drew's bedroom. It was a habit she had acquired once Drew began walking. She had fallen and sprained her wrist when she slipped on the small toys he usually left scattered about the floor.

Cal laid the child on his bed, removing his shoes, socks and outer clothing while Lauren went into an adjoining bath. She returned with a damp cloth and towel, washing away the traces of catsup from his face and hands. Drew stirred, mumbling unintelligibly about the puppies, then settled back to sleep once he was covered with a light-weight cotton blanket.

Lauren turned off the bedside lamp and a night-light glowed, bathing the bedroom in a soft pink glow. She left the room, leaving Cal standing beside the bed.

She walked into her bedroom across the hall and kicked off her pumps. Sitting down on a bentwood rocker, she crossed her legs and waited for Cal. Minutes later he stood in the doorway, hands thrust into the pockets of his trousers.

Lauren sensed his disquiet. "Thank you for dinner."

"It was a bit brief," he said stiffly.

She managed a slight smile. "It was still nice."

He returned her smile. "Do you mind if I come back tomorrow?"

"No, I don't mind, Cal." She gave him a direct stare. "I won't stop you from seeing your son, but I'd prefer you not plan outings that include me. The only thing I ask is that you let me know in advance where you're taking Drew and when you expect to bring him back."

Cal straightened from his leaning position, hands tight-ening into fists. "Is that all, Lauren?"

She nodded. "That's all."

He walked into her bedroom and sat down on a win-dow seat. He ran a hand over the mauve and gray quilt-patterned cushion.

"Well, I have a few things to say." His expression was a mask of stone. "Right now Drew is too young to under-stand what divorce is all about, but there are wounds and scars associated with broken marriages that some children never recover from; besides too many children are grow-ing up not knowing who their fathers are."

Lauren had had more than enough time to plan her

rebuttal when she had replayed this scenario after she discovered she was carrying Caleb Samuels's child.

"It was never my intention to keep Drew from you. If that was my original intent I never would have named you as the father on his birth certificate, and your grandfather wouldn't have been able to prove that Drew was his great-grandson. I'm not that selfish."

"But you're unreasonable," he countered, running all ten fingers through his graying curls, lacing them together at the back of his head.

"Why do you say that?" she asked.

"Because you won't marry me."

Lauren let out her breath in a loud sigh. "Why can't you let it go?" she whispered.

"Damn it, I can't!" His hands came down and curled into tight fists. "I can't, Lauren."

Lauren left the rocker and walked over to stand in front of Cal. For a second, she glimpsed pain. He was hurting.

Sitting down on the window seat, she curbed the urge to hug him. "Why can't you understand . . ."

"I don't want to understand, Lauren," he interrupted. "I married you because I wanted to spend the rest of my life with you."

"Why me and not some other woman?" Lauren questioned, realizing she should've asked Cal the same question when he asked her to marry him on Cay Verde.

He stared down at her upturned face. "Because you were not like any other woman I'd known up to that time. The women I'd . . ." He let his words trail off.

"The women you'd slept with," she finished for him.

"The women I used to see," he insisted. "I never knew if they were with me because they enjoyed my company or whether it was because of who I was.

"It was different with you, Lauren." He reached for her hand and cradled it gently in his larger one. "Do you remember what you said to me the first time we met?"

Her lashes shadowed her eyes. "Yes." Cal pulled her

hand to his chest and she felt the steady, strong pumping of his heart. "I said you didn't have to like me."

"Oh, but I did, Lauren," he confessed. "You were so innocent yet so seductive. And you scared the hell out of me," he also admitted with a wide grin.

Lauren's head came up quickly. "What are you talking about? I was the frightened one. When you asked me to marry you I was too frightened to say no because I didn't want to stop sleeping with you. But you said you wouldn't sleep with me again unless we were married."

He brought her hand to his lips and kissed her fingers. "That's true. And if you hadn't agreed to marry me I would not have slept with you again."

"Why not?"

"Because I didn't want to hurt you. And eventually I would have. You would've returned to Boston and I probably would've continued doing what I had been doing, but it would've always been in the back of my mind that I had taken advantage of you."

What Cal didn't say was that the week he had spent on Cay Verde was magical; she was the magic, and he wasn't willing to let go of the magic. He had thought of her as a beautiful, mythical spirit that had captured him and refused to let him go.

Unconsciously, Lauren laid her cheek against his hard shoulder. "I thought of my stay on Cay Verde in terms of a trip to a fantasy island. I was overwhelmed with the enchantment of the blue skies, turquoise waters, palm trees, exotic flowers, warm trade winds and potent rum drinks. I'd escaped from my humdrum life as a researcher to discover paradise. And in that paradise I encountered the worldly, sybaritic Caleb Samuels. However, that Caleb Samuels was nothing like the rumors I'd heard or the stories I'd read."

Cal felt the electric static of her touch and her warmth. "Don't tell me a woman of your intelligence reads those supermarket rags?" he teased.

Lauren chuckled, pulling away and Cal felt her loss immediately. "Only if I'm on a very long checkout line." She sobered, folding her hands together in her lap. "But the fantasy faded when we came back to the States. It was then that I questioned my sanity. Boston was not Cay Verde, and your grandfather did not welcome me with open arms."

Every muscle in Cal's body tensed. He stared down at her. "What did my grandfather say to you?"

"Nothing."

A frown creased Cal's forehead. "Are you certain?"

"He didn't have to say anything to me, Cal. His not saying anything said it all. He did not approve of your choice in a wife."

Cal relaxed again, pulling Lauren into the circle of his embrace. He felt her stiffen, then relax. "My grandfather was a strange man. He never approved of my father's marriages. And I suppose my mother and Jacqueline gave him reason enough to disapprove of them."

Lauren realized she knew nothing about the private Caleb Samuels. The man she knew was the best-selling author; the jet-setter, the celebrity; the literary genius who had written four bestsellers before he was twenty-eight; he was the man who dated beautiful women, whose photograph had appeared on the cover of *Ebony* and who had been voted one of the beautiful and sexy people for *People* magazine. She had known only one side of Caleb Samuels, and that side she had known intimately.

"What happened to your mother?" she asked softly.

"She's still alive. We share a house in Spain." Cal pulled back, giving her a hopeful smile. "I'd like to take Drew to Spain with me during a holiday."

Lauren's fingers curled into a tight fist against his chest. "I don't know."

He covered her hand with his. "You don't have to give me an answer now." He gave her a sad smile. "There is something I have to tell you, Lauren. Perhaps it'll help you to understand why my grandfather put Drew in his will and why he's forcing us to live together.

"My mother waited until I was seven before she married my father," he began, shocking Lauren with his disclosure. "Even after she married him she refused to live with him. If she was feeling generous, she permitted my father to see me for a weekend or for a few weeks of the summer. There were times when I saw my tutor and the housekeeper more than my parents."

Cal lowered his head and an unnamed emotion flowed from his penetrating eyes. Lauren felt as if he were x-raying her head and her heart, willing her to feel what he was feeling.

"My parents were divorced for the first time when I was ten; two years later they remarried. This union changed all of us when we lived together as a family for the first time. I experienced erratic sleep patterns because I was afraid to go to sleep then wake up to find that I'd been dreaming. It became a dream because three years later it all ended. They divorced for a last and final time and I returned to Barcelona with my mother. The divorce destroyed my father, and he changed, becoming a detached cold stranger to me. I knew he loved me, but he loved my mother more.

"I turned sixteen and my grandfather became the dominant male figure in my life. The times I returned to the States he and I shared fishing trips, baseball and football games and long walks in the snow. Gramps saved me, Lauren. He helped me through the most critical time in my life—adolescence. What I shared with my grandfather I want to share with my son. I want him to come to me when he has a problem he doesn't feel comfortable discussing with you; and I want to help you to help him become the very best that he can be. And because my grandfather didn't want Drew to mirror my life he's forcing us to be together. David Samuels never fought for the right to be my father, but my grandfather wants to make certain I will. Even if he has to do it from his grave."

"You can't accomplish everything in a year," Lauren said, trying to ease the tight fist around her heart.

"We'll begin with a year," he replied quietly. "A year was a lot more than what I was given at Drew's age. If we remarry it won't be for you or me, but for Drew."

Lauren felt attacked by her emotions; twin emotions of desire and fear. She wanted Cal. She wanted his presence and his reminder that she was a woman; a woman who had experienced the full range of her femininity, and she was filled with a fear; a fear that Drew would become a defenseless, hapless victim when she and Cal separated.

She bit down hard on her lower lip. If she gave Cal a year of her life, Lauren knew it would end with one casualty—Lauren Taylor. She couldn't marry him again, then go through the pain of a another separation.

"Think about it, Lauren," Cal said, breaking into her thoughts. "We still have fifty-nine days."

She nodded slowly. "I'll think about it," she promised.

"Do you mind if I take Drew out tomorrow?"

"No . . . no I don't mind." Her head was reeling from Cal's confession.

They sat, side by side, silent, each lost in their private musings. Without warning, Cal stood and glanced down at Lauren. "Good night."

She didn't look up at him. "Good night, Cal." She sat on the window seat until she heard him drive away, then made her way to her attic retreat where she entered her thoughts in a journal. Her small, neat script filled more than four pages. The ink had not dried on the last page when she printed in bold letters what she had printed every day since she began her journal the day after Drew was born: I LOVE CALEB B. SAMUELS II, AND I WILL LOVE HIM FOREVER!

Chapter Six

Lauren had weeded and watered her vegetable garden, fed Missy and put up several loads of wash by the time Cal arrived at eight.

He stood in front of her, holding his arms away from his body. "Better?" He was dressed in a pair of navy chinos, a blue and white striped rugby shirt and a pair of navy blue deck shoes.

Lauren opened the screen door, nodding and admiring his casual attire. "Much better."

His gaze lingered on her shorts, tank top and sandaled feet. "Am I too early?"

"You're just in time for breakfast."

Drew raced across the living room, arms outstretched. "Hi, Daddy."

Cal swung Drew high in the air, then cradled him to his chest. "Hi, partner. What do you have planned for today?"

"I have no plans," Drew whispered in Cal's ear.

"How about a baseball game? The Yankees are in town and perhaps we can see someone blast a few over the Green Monster."

Drew affected a serious expression. "I don't know a Green Monster, Daddy."

Cal pressed his forehead to Drew's. "The Green Monster is the wall at Fenway Park where the Red Sox play baseball."

Drew laughed. "I want to catch a ball, Daddy."

"Drew had better pick up the toys in his room or Drew is going to catch some trouble," Lauren said quietly, watching the interchange between her son and his father.

"Aw, Mommy. Do I have to? I'm only a little kid."

Cal lowered Drew to the floor. "Being a little kid has nothing to do with you not obeying your mother."

Drew pushed out his lower lip, pouting. "I don't know how to put them away," he mumbled.

Cal crossed his arms over his chest. "Do you know how to play with them?"

"They just jump out and play with me," Drew explained, swinging his arms above his head.

"Tell them to jump back into place," Lauren retorted, struggling not to laugh. "You have five minutes, Drew."

Drew gave his father a pleading look. "Daddy, I can't."

"Do it, Drew," Cal ordered in a stern tone.

Lauren and Cal went into the kitchen while Drew stomped up the staircase to his room.

"Is he always this obstinate?" Cal asked.

"Always," Lauren confirmed.

Cal sat down on a tall stool, smiling at Lauren. "He must have inherited his stubbornness from you."

Lauren gripped the handle to a griddle and stared at him. "I suggest you quit while you're still ahead, Caleb."

He held up his hands in a gesture of surrender. "Sorry, ma'am."

Cal watched Lauren as she busied herself preparing breakfast. He had spent the night sorting out all that had happened since seeing her again, and had come to the conclusion that he could not intimidate Lauren. Intimidation fueled her quick temper and she came back at him with everything she could muster and knowing this he decided to romance her; romance her the way he had done on Cay Verde.

His tension eased and a rush of desire, a peaceful, soothing desire swept over him. He would win Lauren's love. She said she had loved him on Cay Verde and he wouldn't stop until she said so again.

Lauren cooked dozens of silver dollar-sized blueberry pancakes, Cal and Drew devouring them as soon as they came off the griddle. She slipped four on a plate for herself and joined them at the table.

"These are the best, Mommy," Drew got out between bites.

Cal nodded in agreement, his mouth full. "You're a fabulous cook, Lauren," he said after swallowing.

"She's the best, Daddy. Mommy makes funny cookies."

Cal raised an eyebrow at Lauren. "What are funny cookies?"

"They are cookies cut into different shapes," she explained. "I usually make them for special occasions."

"My birthday is a special occasion," Drew announced.

Cal smiled, wiggling his eyebrows at Drew. "You're right about that." He drained his second cup of coffee. "Let's clean the kitchen, partner, then we'll head out to the mall before we go to the ballpark."

Drew's jaw dropped as he gasped loudly. "But Mommy cleans the kitchen, Daddy."

"If Mommy cooks, then the men clean."

"But cleaning is for girls," Drew protested.

"Who told you cleaning is for girls?" Cal questioned.

"Tommy's daddy said that only girls clean up."

"Who's Tommy, Lauren?" Cal asked, scowling.

"He lives next door." She glanced across the table at Drew, affecting an expression he was familiar with.

"Let's clean up, Daddy," he said quickly.

Lauren eased off the bench and leaned over Cal. "You

shouldn't have to negotiate, Caleb," she whispered in his ear.

Cal caught her hand, pulling her down to sit beside him. "What do you do?" he whispered back, circling her waist with his right arm.

Lauren felt his hot breath on her neck. The sensual aura that was Caleb Samuels swept over her, battering down her defenses.

"You give him the *look*."

Cal lowered his head, his mouth brushing over her ear. "What's the *look?*"

Her head came up slowly, her mouth only inches from his. Time stood still, then spun out of control, transporting them back to an island where they had escaped party revelers to find their own private sanctuary; a sanctuary filled with primal desire and love.

They had made love in its rawest form: mating.

Cal was hypnotized by the dark fires in Lauren's eyes and the lush moistness of her lips, calling him to taste her succulent fruit over and over.

"It's going to be a while before he can interpret *that* look," Cal said with a knowing smile. "And that won't be until his hormones start running amuck."

Lauren dropped her gaze, charming Cal with the demure gesture. "I'm going to leave you *men* to your chores." He released her and she slid off the bench and walked out of the kitchen.

Moisture had formed between her breasts and her heart was beating rapidly. Inhaling deeply, she made her way up the staircase to her attic retreat. She opened a set of double windows and a light breeze swept into the large space, cooling her fevered flesh.

She wanted Cal and he knew it. There had been no way she could hide it from him.

She flopped down on a daybed, cradling her arms under her head. Maybe if she had slept with another man, any man, after her brief marriage to Caleb Samuels she would have purged him from her system. Perhaps then she would not have the erotic memories that haunted her relentlessly without warning.

Time and time again she relived his breath washing over her moist face, his fingers searching and finding the secret, hidden parts of her body and wringing spasms of desire from her.

Closing her eyes, Lauren could still feel his teeth on her sensitive breasts, biting and suckling them until she thought she was going to lose her mind. She remembered his softly spoken words that calmed her; the soothing voice whose commands she obeyed blindly when he told her to open her mouth and her legs to him.

She opened her eyes, staring up at the pale wallpaper on the ceiling. One year. First it had been one week and now it was one year. Could she afford to give Cal and Drew their year together? Could she afford not to think about what she would gain or lose?

"Lauren?"

She sat up at the sound of the male voice. "I'm over here."

Cal stepped into the attic, glancing around the yawning space. He smiled at her. "Drew said I'd find you up here."

She returned his smile. "This is my inner sanctum."

Cal walked over to a wall of shelves filled from floor to ceiling with books and sheaves of magazines. "When do you work?" he asked, examining the spine of one book.

"Usually at night." Lauren moved off the daybed and joined him at the built-in shelves. "Once Drew's in school I'll change my schedule."

"How many hours do you usually put in each night?"

She shrugged slender shoulders. "It depends on the subject matter and how quickly the material is needed."

Opening a book with a tattered cover, Cal stared at the copyright date. "Will you work for me?"

She remembered the Zulu project. "You don't want me, Cal."

His head snapped up and he stared at her. "Yes I do. I recall being told that you were the best."

"I am good," she replied confidently. "But we don't work well professionally."

"It'll be different this time."

"Why?"

"Both of us are older, more mature, and I don't think we would allow our personal feelings to affect our professionalism."

Lauren knew Cal had spoken the truth. She was older, mature and much more experienced. She wouldn't be so easy to seduce this time.

She nodded. "What do you have in mind?"

A slight smile tilted the corners of his mouth. "I've been toying with a story line ever since Summit offered me the Zulu project. How much do you know about ancient African kingdoms and their religions?"

"North or south of the Sahara?"

"North and south," Cal replied.

Lauren raised her chin, giving him a saucy grin. "Enough."

His eyes brightened in excitement. "Will you do it?"

"Have you put anything down on paper?" she asked, not committing herself. Cal shook his head and Lauren took his arm and directed him across the room. "Come with me."

She led him to a section of the attic where she had set up her computer. She sat down, switching on the screen. Patting the chair beside hers, she smiled up at Cal. "Please sit down." He sat while she booted up the program.

"Talk to me, Cal."

He met her steady gaze. "What about?"

"Your story line."

Cal began, hesitantly at first, then all of the thoughts and ideas he had buried away in the deep recesses of his mind flowed. Lauren typed as quickly as he spoke, his words coming to life as amber letters covered the screen.

Drew entered the attic silently, taking a small stool near the desk. He had learned to sit and wait for his mother to acknowledge him whenever she worked at her computer. He fidgeted, crossing and uncrossing his legs. Patience waning quickly, he left the stool and crawled onto Cal's lap.

Cal held Drew, his plot unraveling slowly but smoothly. As his story unfolded, the tension and uneasiness he had felt whenever he tried writing this novel slipped away. Words he had tried putting into a tape recorder rushed out like a swollen stream.

His voice finally faded and he felt a combination of exhilaration and relief. It was over; his story was out.

Lauren pressed a key, storing the material. Excitement shone from her large, dark eyes. "It's fabulous, Cal."

"I like it too, Daddy," Drew chimed in.

Cal hugged Drew, kissing his forehead. "And I like you too." He tightened his grip on his son, staring over his head at Lauren. Something intense flowed from his entrancement, his gaze slowly appraising her face and body. What he had tried to deny shocked him like a bolt of electricity.

All he had to offer Lauren was a reminder of a week of shared passions on a private tropical island. A week that had changed her life forever.

He had been drawn to Lauren because she was able to touch him the way no woman had been able to do before that time. She continued to touch him, for he had been unable to replace her with other women even after she left him.

He needed her. She was comforting. With her he felt only peace, a peace even when she stubbornly refused to give in to his demands, and guilt nagged his conscience. He needed her, he needed Drew; but did Lauren need him? Her life appeared uncomplicated and filled with predictability. She had a new house to decorate, a young child who looked to her for love and nurturing, and a profession that provided her with security for a comfortable way of life.

Taking a glance at the clock on her desk, Lauren said, "It's after ten. You guys should leave now if you want to go to the mall, then make it to your baseball game."

"Are you coming to Boston with us, Mommy?"

Lauren winked at Drew, trailing her fingers over his smooth cheek. "Not this time, sweetheart."

"Are we going to see Grandma and Grandpa?"

"Grandma and Grandpa are coming over Sunday because Sunday is Father's . . ." Her words trailed off as she realized it would be Cal's first Father's Day celebration. "I'd like you to share dinner with us tomorrow," she said to Cal. "You'll get to meet my parents."

"Good," he replied without hesitating. "I'm looking forward to meeting them."

Drew jumped off Cal's lap. "I'm going to get my baseball cap," he shouted, running out of the attic.

Cal laughed, shaking his head. "Does he ever walk?"

"Never." There was also a trace of laughter in Lauren's voice.

Cal sobered quickly. "I'm very serious about you being the researcher for my book, Lauren. And I prefer not to go through Andrew Monroe."

Lauren knew she had not imagined Cal's resentment of Andrew. "He's my agent, Cal."

He may be your agent but I was your husband, Cal told himself. "I don't want Andrew Monroe involved in this, Lauren, and if you insist on involving him I won't write the book."

Lauren registered the look of implacable determination on his face. "You have to write it." It had been more than five years since C. B. Samuels had released a new book, and the story line for this book was worthy of a Pulitzer. She noted the thinning of Cal's mouth and she knew it was useless to argue with him.

"Okay, Cal. No Andrew," she conceded.

Leaning over, he cradled her face between his hands and kissed her mouth tenderly. "Thank you, darling."

Lauren felt the explosive heat from his mouth and body. It was still alive. The passion had not cooled.

Cal pulled back and stared down into her startled eyes. "You don't realize how special you are, darling. You've given me Drew, so I owe you a gift, Lauren."

She couldn't talk as she nodded numbly. All Caleb Samuels had to do was touch her, kiss her and she was lost. She hadn't matured that much. The man had captured her heart and refused to let it go.

"I'll see you later," Cal said quietly, releasing her and rising to his feet.

"Have a good time." Lauren couldn't control the breathless timbre of her voice.

She sat, wondering if she could take the risk. Could she risk marrying Cal again and come out of the final separation unscathed?

But Lauren knew even if she didn't marry Cal again he would always be in her life. There was no way he was not going to be involved with Drew. He and Drew had bonded quickly and no matter what happened between his parents Drew would have his father.

The phone rang and Lauren answered the call. It was Andrew Monroe, telling her he had received her latest packet of material. Andrew did not mention Caleb Samuels and neither did Lauren before he hung up. Andrew Monroe was the only person, aside from her family, who knew who Drew's father was.

Intuition told Lauren that Cal did not like Andrew and the feeling was mutual, and she was caught in the middle. Her love for Andrew was a special love. He was a friend, a confidant she loved, but she was not in love with him. He had become a protector—for her and Drew and the love that had developed between the three of them was one of closeness and family.

Thinking of family, she called her mother, informing Odessa that Cal would join them for their Father's Day celebration. She hung up, sighing audibly. She had to find something suitable for a Father's Day gift for her son's father.

Chapter Seven

Drew arrived home asleep in Cal's arms, and Lauren overrode the child's feeble protests when she gave him a bath, washing away the distinctive odor of mustard and popcorn.

Dressed in cotton pajamas, Drew groped for his bed and was sound asleep before Lauren turned off the light and joined Cal in the kitchen.

Cal sat at the table, drinking a cup of freshly brewed coffee. Lauren gave him a warm smile. "Drew's one tired little boy."

"Make that one tired little boy and one very tired daddy," Cal admitted, returning her smile with a strained one of his own.

Lauren filled a cup with coffee and added a splash of milk. "It's going to take a while before you adjust to parenting," she said, using her hip to close the refrigerator door. She walked over to the dining nook and sat down opposite Cal. "But for you the worst is over. Feedings at 3:00 A.M., and teething can test the limits of one's sanity."

Cal stared at her from under heavy eyelids. "I missed everything that was important, Lauren. I missed you telling me that I was going to be a father. I missed seeing my son's birth, and because of you I missed all of the important milestones."

His voice was void of emotion and it chilled Lauren,

and at that moment she felt as if he could hate her. His gaze shifted to his cup, searching its black depths for answers she could not give him.

"I'm sorry, Cal," she apologized in a quiet voice. "But I can't spend the rest of my life atoning for doing what I thought was the right thing to do at that time."

Cal raised his head, peering intently at her strained expression. "You'll make it up to me," he stated flatly. "I'll make certain of that," he added, rising to his feet.

Lauren watched him walk to the sink and empty the remains of his coffee into it. He rinsed the cup and placed it in the dishwasher. There was a pregnant silence, the absence of sound oppressive.

She knew she had wounded him, and he was angry because she walked out on him. She had trampled Caleb Samuels's male pride because she had left him after being married for only two days. It was only now, after two days, that she saw a man who was very different from the one she had met on Cay Verde.

Which man was the real Caleb Samuels? This one was more of a stranger than the one she'd met on Cay Verde. She had married him, borne his child, and still he was a stranger.

"What time is dinner tomorrow?" he questioned, managing to display a polite smile.

Lauren's composure was as fragile as an eggshell and she exhibited a calm she did not feel. "Three. It's very informal. Weather permitting we'll eat outdoors."

Cal nodded, running a hand over his hair. His fingers lingered on his neck, massaging the tight muscles. "Do you need my help with anything?"

"No thank you." She wanted him away from her, out of her house. His presence had become too unsettling and disturbing.

"Good night, Cal," she said, dismissing him.

Cal's fatigue vanished quickly when he realized Lauren had again unceremoniously asked him to leave. The frustration he had experienced when he sat in John Evans's office and saw his ex-wife again threatened to swallow him whole.

He loved her; he hated her; then he loved her again, and he wanted her; he wanted to take her in his arms, take her to his bed and bury himself in her moist heat.

Lauren was frustrating and an enigma. She wasn't as worldly or sophisticated as the other women he had known yet she was more uninhibited and generous than all of the others combined, and with her innocence she had given him the chance for a rebirth, a renewal of his spirit and his flesh.

With the renewal she had given him a child—his son.

"Good night, Lauren." Without another word he turned, walking out of the kitchen and out of the house.

Lauren waited before making her way to the front door. She stared out at the shadowy twilight, trying to belay her quiet anxiety; an anxiety that indicated she wanted Caleb Samuels back in her life; she wanted to live with Caleb Samuels—as husband and wife.

Sitting down on the cushioned softness of the white wicker love seat, she pulled her legs up under her body.

Cal's passionate confession came to mind. *My mother waited until I was seven before she married my father. Even after she married him she refused to live with him.*

"Why?" Lauren asked the encroaching nightfall. Why did Cal's mother wait so long to marry his father? Why had she refused to live with David Samuels? Why was Drew's life mirroring that of his father's? She had so many questions and no answers to those questions.

She shifted her legs, and a small object fell to the porch. "Drew," she mumbled. It was probably another one of his numerous little trucks. Leaning over, Lauren picked up a gaily wrapped square package.

There was still enough light to read the tiny tag attached to a streamer of white ribbon: HAPPY MOTHER'S DAY.

Her hands were steady as she stripped the pale blue paper from a navy blue velvet box. The gift was from Tiffany's. Lauren recalled Cal's *I owe you a gift.*

She opened the box, staring numbly at a bracelet. Now her hands were shaking as she retreated to the living room and examined the heavy bangle under the light of a floor lamp. His gift to her was a three-tiered gold circle of precious stones.

She snapped the bracelet of ruby baguettes, banded by twin rows of round diamonds, around her wrist. Blood-red sensual rubies and brilliant blue-white diamonds winked back at her.

Lauren removed the bracelet, replacing it in the box and holding it to her chest.

He didn't owe her anything. Cal had given her love, joy and Drew. Nothing he could ever buy for her could equal the love, joy and Drew.

"Oh, I love him" Lauren whispered. Her hands shook slightly as she bit down hard on her lower lip.

Her mind burned with the memories of Cay Verde and she wanted to relive the week over and over again—with Cal. But, she pondered, could they relive the experience if they remarried? Had the separation changed them so much that they wouldn't be able to recapture the tenderness and trust to survive the year they were forced to remain together?

Lauren was aware that Cal loved and trusted her on Cay Verde, but she was not so naïve to believe that he still loved her after she deceived him. She knew he wanted her—he had always wanted her the way she had wanted him and continued to want him.

I want him in my life *now!* There, she had admitted it herself. She hadn't thought that Drew needed his father for at that moment she thought only of herself.

She felt a bottomless peace, knowing she needed to share her joy with someone. Within minutes she made a call, then waited for the one person who had taunted her for years to release the demons who had tormented her since she returned from Cay Verde bearing Caleb Baldwin Samuels's name while unknowingly carrying his child in her womb.

Gwendolyn Taylor sat on the daybed, her legs tucked under her body, eyes wide in surprise. "If you're asking me to be your maid of honor, then you must be getting married. But to whom? Where *is* he, cuz? I've never seen you with a man since you've come back from that Caribbean island or—wait—don't tell me you and Andrew . . ." Her words trailed off as Lauren shook her head.

"It's not Andrew, Gwen."

Gwen's large dark eyes grew rounder as her mouth formed a perfect O. "Who?"

"Caleb Samuels." Lauren couldn't believe she could sound so calm while her heart pounded uncontrollably.

Gwen screamed and the first cousins fell into each other's arms, hugging and crying at the same time.

Lauren and Gwendolyn were first cousins, born within weeks of each other and closer than sisters. The resemblance between them was striking, and many people thought they were siblings. Gwen was an inch taller and her body slightly fuller than Lauren's, and both of them wore their hair short and curling.

Gwen patted her chest with a manicured hand, exhaling heavily. "Now that's what I call headline news."

"Don't you dare print a word of this until I make it official." Gwen's *People, Home,* and *Style* column was a popular feature of the *Boston Gazette.* The *Gazette* offered a refreshing change from the *Boston Globe* and *Boston Herald* reporting. It featured news on a hometown scale, focusing on local personalities and places of interest.

Gwen frowned. "Why isn't it official?"

Lauren rested her elbows on her knees crossed in a

yoga position. "I haven't told Cal that I would marry him again."

"And why not?"

Lauren revealed everything that had happened since she'd received the letter requesting her presence at the reading of Dr. Caleb Samuels's will. "All I have to do is marry Cal, live with him for a year and Drew will inherit his share of his great-grandfather's estate."

"And if you don't, Jackie Samuels will get it," Gwen stated, an expression of astonishment still apparent in her eyes.

"That is the stipulation," Lauren confirmed.

"What do you know about Jackie Samuels, cuz?"

Lauren shrugged her shoulders. "Nothing, except that Cal doesn't want her to get a penny from his grandfather's estate."

"I've never met your C. B. Samuels, but I have to agree with him, Lauren," she said soberly. "I've heard that Jackie Samuels is a first-class b-i-t-c-h. I remember reading about her when she broke up a liaison David Samuels was having with a woman he'd been seeing for years. He and the woman were engaged to be married, but once Jackie arrived on the scene the woman was history— ancient history."

Closing her eyes, Lauren knew she had to act and act fast. She had to protect Drew's inheritance. Opening her eyes, she stared at Gwen, and the other woman recognized the stubborn streak in Lauren by the set of her delicate jaw.

"Can you do me a favor, Gwen?"

"Sure, cuz, anything."

"Find out everything you can about Jacqueline Samuels."

Gwen patted Lauren's hand. "Give me a few days to check the morgue at the *Gazette*. If I can't find anything there, then I'll call someone at the *Globe* or *Herald*. Now, how about we toast this most wonderful news?" she suggested, lightening the mood.

Lauren sprang to her feet, smiling. "Excellent idea."

"Do you love him?" Gwen asked as Lauren made her way across the room.

Turning slowly, Lauren gave her cousin an incredulous look. "Of course I love him, Gwen. Why do you think I'm remarrying him?"

It was Gwen's turn to shrug her shoulders. "I don't know. I thought maybe you were doing it because of Drew."

"No, Gwen. It's not because of Drew. I'm doing it for the same reason I married Cal in the first place—love. There was a time when I thought I'd married him because I was caught up in an idealistic romanticism and a physical attraction so strong that I thought it was infatuation—one set of glands calling to another. I went through periods of insecurity, feeling excited and eager, but not genuinely happy. I had nagging doubts, unanswered questions and there were things about Cal I should've known but never knew. All I knew was that he was this incredibly gentle, passionate stranger who swept me off my feet the moment I met him.

"But the separation changed me, Gwen, because now I'm calmer, patient and willing to give our marriage a chance to work. My life is going the way I want it to go. I have a career I love, the house I've always wanted, and a wonderful son, and marrying Cal will complete the circle."

Gwen arched her eyebrows. "So you're ready to settle and play house, cuz?"

Lauren rested her hands on her hips. "You just watch me work it, cuz!"

"What I want to watch is C. B. Samuels in the flesh," Gwen countered.

"You'll get to meet him, Gwen."

"When?"

"Next week."

Gwen pushed out her lower lip in a pout. "Do you think he'll give me an interview?"

"Cal doesn't grant interviews." This was something Lauren *did* know about the man she was going to remarry.

Gwen nodded in resignation. "Go get the champagne so we can toast your upcoming nuptials."

Lauren and Gwen spent the next two hours talking and sipping champagne, laughing uncontrollably when they recounted the pranks they'd played on unsuspecting friends growing up.

It was past midnight and Gwen turned down Lauren's offer to spend the night, explaining she had scheduled an interview with a local musician over Sunday brunch.

"Who knows," Gwen threw over her shoulder as she stood on the porch with Lauren, "maybe I'll be lucky enough to see the sex muffin again. The next time it won't be because I'm on assignment."

Lauren hugged her cousin. "Thanks for being my maid of honor."

"I'm honored you asked. I'll call if I get any information on Jackie Samuels."

Lauren waited until her cousin drove away, then returned to the house. She had made her decision. She would remarry Caleb Samuels, live with him a year and fulfill the terms of Dr. Samuels's will.

Gramps had won the first round.

"Mommy! Mommy! Daddy's here."

Lauren heard Drew's strident voice coming through the open windows. He's early, she thought, glancing up at the clock over the sink. It was only two-thirty.

Cal walked into the kitchen with a grace not seen on most men, except dancers. Head erect, shoulders thrown back and his slim hips rolling in a sensually fluid motion, he always managed to turn heads wherever he went.

We've got your authors!

If you seek out the latest historical romances by today'
bestselling authors, our new reader's service, KENSINGTON
CHOICE, is the club for you.

KENSINGTON CHOICE is the only club where you can fin
authors like Janelle Taylor, Shannon Drake, Rosanne Bittner, Sylv
Sommerfield, Penelope Neri and Phoebe Conn all in one place...

...and the only service that will deliver their romances direct t
your home as soon as they are published—even before they reach th
bookstores.

KENSINGTON CHOICE is also the only service that wi
give you a substantial guaranteed discount off the publisher's pric
on every one of those romances.

That's right: Every month, the Editors at Zebra and Pinnac
select four of the newest novels by our bestselling authors and rus
them straight to you, usually *before they reach the bookstores.* Th
publisher's prices for these romances range from $4.99 to $5.99—b
they are always yours for the guaranteed low price of just *$4.20!*

That means you'll always save over 20%...often as much
30%...off the publisher's prices on every shipment you get fro
KENSINGTON CHOICE!

All books are sent on a 10-day free examination basis, and the
is no minimum number of books to buy. (A postage and handli
charge of $1.50 is added to each shipment.)

As your introduction to the convenience and value of this ne
service, we invite you to accept

4 BOOKS FREE

The 4 books, worth up to
$23.96, are our welcoming gift.
You pay only $1 to help cover
postage and handling.

To start your subscription
to KENSINGTON CHOICE
and receive your introductory
package of 4 FREE romances,
detach and mail the postpaid
card at right *today.*

We have 4 FREE BOOKS for you as your introduction to KENSINGTON CHOICE
To get your FREE BOOKS, worth up to $23.96, mail the card below.

FREE BOOK CERTIFICATE

As my introduction to your new KENSINGTON CHOICE reader's service, please send me 4 FREE historical romances (worth up to $23.96), billing me just $1 to help cover postage and handling. As a KENSINGTON CHOICE subscriber, I will then receive 4 brand-new romances to preview each month for 10 days FREE. I can return any shipment within 10 days and owe nothing. The publisher's prices for the KENSINGTON CHOICE romances range from $4.99 to $5.99, but as a subscriber I will be entitled to get them for just $4.20 per book or $16.80 for all four titles. There is no minimum number of books to buy, and I can cancel my subscription at any time. A $1.50 postage and handling charge is added to each shipment.

Name _____

Address _____ Apt. _____

City _____ State _____ Zip _____

Telephone (___) _____

Signature _____
(If under 18, parent or guardian must sign)

Subscription subject to acceptance. Terms and prices subject to change.

KC0195

His walk was something she recognized immediately when she first met him on Cay Verde.

Everything about Caleb Samuels was measured and unhurried. Each word he spoke and each motion he made. She remembered that even his lovemaking had been slow, methodical and unhurried, sending her beyond herself and spewing a flood-tide of explosive pleasure.

The muscles in her stomach contracted when she thought about making love to him; seeing him, touching him, had brought back the vivid memories. Each time he touched her she was certain he could feel her trembling hunger.

His gaze went to her bare wrists, then moved slowly up to her face. He handed her two decorative shopping bags.

"I didn't know what you were serving so I brought red and white wine."

Lauren wiped her hands on a towel, smiling. "Both are appropriate. I'm serving red meat and poultry." She took the bags from him, her fingers brushing his, and Cal pulled away as if he had been burned.

The air was radiating with tension—sexual and emotional as she concealed a mysterious smile. "I've decided to marry you," Lauren announced softly.

Cal stood motionless in the middle of the kitchen, breathing heavily through parted lips. She had given in. It was so easy, too easy to digest all at once.

"Why, Lauren?" Cal chided himself as soon as the words were out. She had accepted; why did he want to know why?

Lauren turned back to cutting up the vegetables for a garden salad, unable to look at Cal. "I'm doing it for Drew," she lied.

At that moment Cal didn't care why she had decided to marry him again—all that mattered was that she had agreed to do it. He reached for her, cradling her gently in the circle of his embrace. She stiffened slightly before she melted against the solid hardness of his body.

Lauren curved her arms around Cal's waist, resting her cheek against his chest. It felt good, so natural to be in his arms. She had not realized how much she had missed his touch, his warmth.

She raised her face, smiling up at him. "You're going to have to let me go so I can finish cooking."

Cal caught her chin between his thumb and forefinger. His gaze lingered longingly on her face, focusing on her mouth. His head descended slowly and he staked his claim in a slow, drugging kiss.

Lauren rose on tiptoe, her arms going around his neck. She moaned softly as his tongue traced the outline of her mouth seconds before his teeth sank tenderly into her lower lip.

Cal devoured her mouth, and an explosive heat swept through Lauren; a sexual heat she had not felt in years.

It wasn't for Drew. She had consented to remarry Caleb Samuels because she still was in love with him—she had never stopped loving him.

Lauren pushed against his chest and he released her. Both of them were breathing heavily.

Cheeks flaming, she glanced away. "I have to finish the salad," she mumbled, not recognizing the sound of her own voice.

"I'll see about Drew," Cal offered as an excuse before walking out of the kitchen.

Lauren prepared all of the fixings for her salad, then retreated to her bedroom to change her clothes. She took a quick shower and pulled a white sundress with narrow straps, a loose waistline and a swingy skirt over her perfumed, scented body. She slipped her bare feet into a pair of white leather sandals at the same time she heard her parents' car pull into the driveway.

Skipping lightly down the staircase, Lauren met her mother and father as they were coming up the porch. She hugged her father, kissing his cheek and pushing an envelope with a gift certificate to a sporting-goods store into his hand. "Happy Father's Day, Daddy."

Roy Taylor curved an arm around his daughter's waist. "Thank you, princess." He stared down at the envelope. "You didn't have to give me anything, Lauren."

Lauren smiled up at Roy. "I know I didn't, but I wanted to." She kissed her mother, looping an arm through Odessa's. "Cal's here," she informed her.

Odessa looked over Lauren's shoulder. "Where is he?"

"Probably around the back with Drew."

Lauren led her parents along the path to the rear of the large house. She spied Cal and Drew on a webbed lounge chair, the child sitting between his father's outstretched legs as Cal read the colorful Sunday comics.

Cal saw Lauren and her parents approaching, and he eased Drew off the chair and stood up. He noted that Lauren had not inherited her mother's looks. However, the two women shared the same graceful body.

He stared at Lauren as if seeing her for the first time. Seeing her in the sundress brought back the vivid reminder of the evening he had met her on the beach on Cay Verde and had apologized for insulting her because of her youthful-looking appearance. Even though her hair was shorter and the dress a different color, Lauren had an aura of feminine sensuality that still aroused him.

Lauren stood beside Cal, looping a bare arm through his. "Cal, I'd you to meet my parents. Odessa and Roy. Mama, Daddy, this is Caleb Samuels."

Cal extended his right hand to Roy Taylor. "My pleasure, Mr. Taylor."

Roy pumped his hand vigorously. "Roy will be enough, Caleb."

Cal turned to Odessa, lowering his head slightly and giving her a sensual smile. "I'm honored, Mrs. Taylor."

Odessa's cheeks colored under the heat of his golden-eyed gaze. "Odessa," she said breathlessly.

Taking a step forward, Cal leaned down and kissed her smooth, scented cheek. "Odessa," he repeated.

Lauren exhaled, her heart thumping uncomfortably. She didn't know what to expect from her parents.

Odessa gave Cal her winning smile, but there was a look in her eyes that Lauren recognized immediately and she tensed.

"I hope you're not returning to Spain at the end of the summer, because I'd hate for my grandson to get used to you, then have to miss you."

Lauren bit down on her lower lip, shaking her head. Her mother was notorious for being facetious, however, Cal seemed amused by her statement.

"I'm not going anywhere for a long time," he stated solemnly, staring down at Lauren.

Odessa arched her eyebrows. She was stopped from interrogating Cal further when Drew caught her hand. "Grandma, come see the puppies. Missy had puppies. You too, Grandpa."

The elder Taylors followed Drew to the garage to view the puppies while Lauren and Cal stared at each other.

His eyes crinkled in a smile. "I see where you get your incredible beauty from. Your mother is stunning."

Lauren laughed. "You lie so nicely, Cal. I look nothing like my mother."

He sobered quickly. "Beauty is not about looks, Lauren. It's one's inner spirit that radiates beauty, not one's face. A perfect example is Jacqueline. She's as wicked inwardly as she is beautiful facially."

"Wicked stepmothers only exist in fairy tales, Cal."

"Well, this one lives and breathes. And with Jacqueline, your first line of defense is never to underestimate her as your opponent."

"Jacqueline Samuels is not my opponent," Lauren argued.

Cal let out a sigh of exasperation, his lips compressed

in a grim, tight line. "Just watch yourself, Lauren." He stared at her intently.

Lauren digested his warning, not wanting to believe she had anything to fear from Jacqueline Samuels, but something nagged at her despite her confidence.

Remembering Cal's gift, she pulled a small velvet pouch from the large pocket in her dress. "Happy Father's Day, Caleb."

He took the pouch and shook out the contents. The heavy gold ring he had given Lauren was cradled in the palm of his large hand. She had returned the ring he had given her when they married. Lauren took the ring from his palm and slipped it on the little finger of his left hand.

He captured her eyes with his, seemingly undressing her. He was remembering the time he had slipped the ring on her finger.

Gathering her in his arms, he held her gently, rocking her back and forth. "Thank you, darling," he whispered in her hair.

Lauren felt her breasts tighten and swell against his chest. Cradled in his embrace she mentally relived making love with Cal.

Closing her eyes, she inhaled his masculine scent, felt the whisper of his breath over the planes and curves of her stomach and thighs; she felt the moistness of his tongue as it trailed along her inner thigh and over the dark, moist mound concealing her womanhood; she relived his strong fingers cupping her breasts gently, thumbs stroking her distended nipples, and she relived his tongue plunging deeply into her mouth over and over, drinking the sweet ambrosia she willingly offered him.

Her husband; her patient, sensual husband.

But he was not her husband—not yet.

Lauren was smiling when she opened her eyes. She was to become Mrs. Caleb Samuels for the second time in less than five years. How many women were fortunate enough to marry the man they loved, not once but twice?

Chapter Eight

The mood was relaxed and lively for the Father's Day dinner; savory strips of butterfly lamb and split Cornish hens were cooked to perfection on the gas grill. The accompanying side dishes included egg noodles with a mustard-sage sauce, a garden salad and another salad of lobster and artichoke hearts with a lemon dressing.

Drew's excitement was endless. He reveled in the praise from both of his grandparents as he ate everything on his plate.

Lauren stared at Cal over the rim of her wineglass, feeling as if she had known him for years rather than a sum total of ten days. He appeared so at ease with her parents, while the elder Taylors seemed comfortable and friendly with the stranger who had once been married to their daughter.

Lauren caught Odessa's eye, smiling. Her gaze shifted to Cal and he returned her smile. They had decided to wait until dinner was completed to announce their marriage.

"Mama, Daddy, Cal and I have decided to get married."

Odessa's mouth dropped, snapped closed, then dropped again. "When?"

"Next month," Cal replied.

"When next month?" Odessa asked, placing a hand to her throat.

"Either the last Saturday in July or the first Saturday in August," Lauren stated. She and Cal would have a month to become acquainted before living together.

Odessa crossed her arms under her breasts. "You're not giving me much time. I have to send out invitations, mail announcements to the newspapers, order flowers, food and arrange for the church."

"No, Mother!"

Odessa's eyes suddenly filled with tears. "Indulge me, Lauren. Please, baby. Just this one time. I didn't get to see you married the first time. You cheated me out of seeing my only child married," she wailed, her chin trembling.

Roy pulled Odessa to his body and kissed her forehead. His wife sniffled dramatically against his shoulder as he murmured softly in her ear.

Lauren felt as if her composure were under attack. She couldn't deal with all of the emotions bombarding her. She was unable to shake off Cal's warning about Jacqueline, her mother resorting to tears to get her way, and her father glaring at her as if she were an enemy for upsetting his wife.

She glanced over at Cal and saw him watching her, his forehead furrowed in concern. He nodded and she knew what she had to do.

"Okay, Mama. But I want it small and very private."

Odessa's crying stopped immediately. Turning, she smiled at Lauren and Cal. "Small and private," she repeated.

Sighing heavily, Lauren returned Odessa's smile. "We'll talk about it tomorrow."

Drew helped Cal and Roy clear the table while Lauren and Odessa brewed coffee and sliced a freshly prepared strawberry shortcake for dessert.

Odessa noted Lauren's impassive expression. "It's going to work out, darling," she whispered softly, then turned and retreated to the patio, carrying the carafe of steaming coffee.

Closing her eyes, Lauren gripped the edge of the counter tightly. She felt like a hypocrite. She was to take the vows of matrimony yet knowing every word she'd utter would be false; false and empty.

Love and cherish, in sickness and in health.

But she did love Caleb Samuels. Opening her eyes, she stared at him as he stood with Roy loading the dishwasher.

Lauren had always been honest with herself and she knew her feelings for Cal were changing, intensifying. She looked forward to seeing him, hearing his voice and having him touch her.

He turned and caught her staring and his golden gaze held her captive. Could he see beneath her controlled exterior to feel her apprehension? Could he see her hope that after she married him his feelings toward consistency her would change? Could she hope that he wanted to marry her again for the same reason he had married her on Cay Verde? Could he see her hope that this marriage did not have to end after a year?

Cal mumbled an apology to Roy and crossed the kitchen. He didn't know how or why, but he knew Lauren was uneasy about something. It was as if her inner spirit called out to him to help her.

Reaching for her hands, he held them firmly, tightening his grip when he felt them tremble. "Are you all right?"

Lauren nodded, not meeting his gaze, and tried unsuccessfully to extract her fingers. "I'm fine," she managed in a husky voice.

Cal lowered his head. "You don't look okay."

Lauren felt her apprehension spiral. Could he also sense what she was feeling? Did she know that she wanted him? Wanted him the way a woman wanted a man? The way a wife would want her husband?

"I'm just a little tired," she admitted, and she was. She had pushed herself relentlessly the past two months. Decorating the house, taking care of Drew and compiling research had left her exhausted.

Cal's arms went around her shoulders, holding her protectively against his body. He pressed a light kiss to her forehead.

"I think we should consider a honeymoon."

"Honeymoon!" Lauren practically shouted.

He gave her a warm smile. "Yes, honeymoon."

Odessa reentered the kitchen from the patio. She watched Cal cradle Lauren's face between his palms and drop a kiss on her pouting lips.

"It's settled," he stated in a firm tone. "We'll take a week off and relax."

Lauren's fingers curled around his strong wrists. "But I can't afford to take a week off. I have a project to complete for Andrew. Who's going to watch Drew? And there's Missy and the puppies."

"Your mother can take care of Drew. When my mother comes for the wedding she can extend her stay for a week and take care of Missy and the dogs if you don't want the animals in a kennel."

Lauren squinted up at Cal, not seeing her parents watching the tense interchange. She shook her head. "No, Caleb."

His hands held her head firmly, not permitting her movement. "Yes, Lauren." His eyes darkened and grew cold. "I need you healthy and sane for the next year. I lost you once. And I swear it will not happen a second time," he said so quietly that only Lauren heard the veiled promise.

She felt an icy chill grip her. "Take your hands off me," she ordered in a soft voice.

Cal released her, but not before he kissed her for the

second time that day, leaving her mouth burning with a
fire that ignited her whole body.

Odessa and Roy exchanged knowing glances. Both of
them turned and made their way to the patio, Odessa
holding Drew's hand and pulling him with her. There
were a lot of things his mother and father had to work out,
and it was better that they were left alone to do it.

Lauren pulled the back of her hand across her mouth
as if to wipe away any trace of the taste of Cal's lips on
hers.

The gesture amused him. He leaned forward to kiss her
again and she ducked under his arm.

"Stop, Caleb!" Her protest sounded weak even to her
own ears.

Cal caught her arm, spinning her around to face him.
"Stop running from me."

"I'm not running from you," she protested.

He pulled her up close to his chest, frowning as she
closed her eyes. "Are you afraid of me, Lauren?"

Opening her eyes, Lauren prayed he would not feel her
slight trembling. She wasn't afraid of him; she was afraid
of herself and what she felt whenever he looked at her or
touched her.

Raising her chin, she managed a sensual smile. "No,
Cal. I'm not afraid of you." At that moment she wasn't.
Not with her parents less than fifty feet away.

What he didn't know was that she was afraid of herself;
afraid of what she felt whenever he touched her; afraid
she would blurt out her love for him; afraid that he would
reject her love the way she had rejected his love.

Cal smiled and released her. "If what you say is true,
then I'd like you to have your parents babysit Drew tomorrow night."

"Why?" His request gnawed at Lauren's new-found
confidence.

"We haven't spent any time together—alone."

Nervously, she bit her lower lip. "There's no need to be alone."

A look of implacable determination filled Cal's eyes. "I beg to differ with you, Lauren. There are a lot of things we must discuss before we remarry."

Lauren knew he was right. There were a lot of things to discuss and a lot questions to be answered. "Okay, Cal. I'll ask my mother if she'll take care of Drew."

Cal lingered in the kitchen after Lauren retreated to the patio. He needed time alone to regain his composure.

The more he saw of Lauren the more he wanted to see her. He couldn't help himself when he kissed her; he wanted to kiss her again and again—all over her body. *Be careful,* he warned himself. It would be disastrous if he found himself so much in love with his beautiful little wife that he wouldn't let her go after a year, because he was enough of a realist not to think beyond the year with Lauren. She was marrying him for Drew, not because she loved him, a fact he could not afford to forget.

Cal made his way out of the house, joining the Taylors and devouring the strawberry shortcake Lauren had made earlier that morning.

For once, Odessa was speechless when Lauren asked her if she would look after Drew Monday night. She quickly agreed and cradled Drew on her lap where they both made plans about what they intended to do together.

Roy gathered Lauren to his side, pressing a kiss to her forehead. "Thanks for the gift certificate and for the lamb, baby girl."

Lauren wound her arms around her father's thickening waist. "Anytime, Daddy." She patted his slightly protruding belly. "You're putting on weight," she told her college-administrator father. "Sitting at a desk is telling on you."

"I'll have to walk three miles tomorrow just to offset those two slices of shortcake."

Rising on tiptoe, Lauren kissed his cheek. "Get Mama to walk with you."

Roy Taylor's black eyes swept over his wife's willowy figure. Odessa, a retired school librarian, was as slim as she was when he first married her thirty years ago. "There's nothing wrong with Dessa's body. She's perfect."

Lauren was surprised to see the obvious flames of desire in her father's eyes as he stared at her mother. It was something she would never experience with Cal at her parents' age.

"Cardiovascular, Dad."

"And there's nothing wrong with Dessa's heart," he said softly.

"Case closed," Lauren conceded with a smile.

Lauren, Drew, and Cal walked the elder Taylors to their car and watched until it disappeared from view.

"Drew! Drew! Can I see the puppies?" shouted a high-pitched childish voice from the neighboring house.

Drew grasped Lauren's hand. "Mommy, can I show Tommy the puppies?"

She smiled at the excitement flickering in his gold-brown eyes. "Yes. But the two of you stay in the garage, and remind Tommy not to get too close to Missy."

"Thanks, Mommy. See you later, Daddy . . ." Drew was already racing around to the side of the house.

Lauren stood beside Cal, staring out at the verdant lushness of the thick green grass sloping down to the road. Ribbons of sunlight filtered through towering trees throwing lengthening shadows on every light surface. In another two hours dusk would begin its quiet, soothing descent on North Grafton.

Cal threaded his fingers through Lauren's, leading her back to the porch. He seated her on the wicker swing, sitting down next to her and winding an arm around her shoulders.

Lauren melted against his chest, savoring his warmth and masculine strength. Her lids fluttered closed when he brushed her forehead with a light kiss.

A low chuckle filled Cal's chest. "Be careful, love. We're beginning to act like an old married couple rocking on the porch after dinner."

"You're old, Caleb," Lauren teased in a drowsy voice, opening her eyes. "You're the one with the white hair."

His fingers tightened around the slender column of her neck. "It's silver," he corrected softly.

"And that makes you old."

He smiled. "How old?"

"Just too old."

"Too old for what?" he asked against her hair. When she didn't answer, he curved a hand under her chin and raised her face to his. "Too old for what, darling?"

A delicious shudder heated Lauren's body under his penetrating gaze. She wanted so much for their upcoming marriage to be a normal one. But it was not to be.

"Nothing," she finally replied.

Cal settled her cheek on his chest and stared up at the differing shades streaking the sky. A satisfied smile touched his mobile mouth. He certainly wasn't too old to make love to a woman; especially if that woman was Lauren.

Cradling her soft body, inhaling her sweet feminine scent and tasting her velvety lush lips was like an aphrodisiac.

At twenty-seven Lauren Taylor was all woman and he tried remembering if she had been that alluring at twenty-two. Had he been able to sense the essence of her womanliness because he lived so jaded an existence?

Caleb B. Samuels II always took responsibility for his mistakes, and he had made a mistake to let Lauren go five years ago. It would not happen again. He would marry her again, but he would not let her go so easily a second time.

Lauren slipped off her sandals, pulling her legs up under her body. Relaxing, she gave in to the gentle swaying of the porch swing. Aside from her attic retreat, the porch was her favorite place in the large, airy farmhouse. Its wide proportions were perfect for the all-weather white wicker love seat, chaise, tea cart and swing. Brilliant flowering fuchsia, hanging from clay pots and two large window boxes filled with colorful impatiens blended with the pale blue seat cushions and pillows dotted with a delicate pink and white floral print.

She was content to sit with Cal and rock in silence, savoring the quiet of the early Sunday evening, the cool breezes sweeping the countryside, and the comfortable peace Caleb Samuels offered her.

It was a scene she had dreamt of as a girl: a husband, wife and child sharing their love and enjoying their home.

Get real, Lauren, she told herself. She had the child, the house and she was going to gain a husband who was a stranger; a man she had slept with; a man she had married; a man who had stirred the passions she hadn't known she possessed, and a man she would marry and lose again within a year.

There was so much she wanted to know about him. There were so many questions that needed answers. "Cal."

"Yeah?"

"Your mother."

"What about her?" he asked drowsily.

"Why did she wait so long to marry your father?" Cal laughed and the sound startled Lauren. "What's so funny?"

"My parents. They were the most mismatched couple that ever existed. My mother was a brilliant, temperamental dancer and my father was a rigid, controlling attorney whose specialty was the entertainment business—the stage and recordings. They were complete opposites yet they couldn't stay away from each other. There was so much passion between them that to be in the same room with them was tiring. It wasn't until I was older that I realized some people can love to an excess. My father loved me, Lauren, but he loved my mother so much more. And his love smothered her and she fought him. They fought without uttering a word by hurling smoldering glares at each other and these were the times when I wanted to run away and hide. I retreated to a world of books and by the time I was nineteen I knew I wanted to be a writer. My first book was published at twenty-one, and every time I began a new book it was like retreating all over again."

Lauren stared up at his stoic expression. "It's been a long time between books, C.B."

Cal kissed the end of her nose. "This one is going to be different, Lauren."

"Why?"

Cal didn't get the chance to answer as the sound of a car's engine shattered the quietness of the evening. Lauren sat up when she felt tension tighten Cal's body. Andrew was out of his car and striding up the walk before she extracted herself from Cal's embrace.

Andrew whistled off-key as he bounded up the steps, smiling broadly. Lauren returned his smile, not seeing the scowl Cal shot her agent.

Andrew extended his hand to Cal. "Hello."

Cal rose slowly to his feet and shook the proffered hand. He resented Andrew; he resented his unannounced intrusion and he resented his close relationship with Lauren.

"Good evening, Monroe," Cal returned in a stilted tone. He couldn't address him as Andrew. The name was too close to his son's, and that only reminded him that Andrew Monroe had solidified his influence not only in Lauren's life but also Drew's.

Lauren looped her arm through Andrew's after he released Cal's hand. The smile she offered him mirrored her deep affection for the man who was her agent and friend.

Leaning over, Andrew brushed a light kiss on her cheek. "I'm sorry I didn't call, but . . ."

"You didn't call because you hate telephones," Lauren teased, placing a small manicured hand on his chest. "Please sit down." She gestured toward the love seat.

She retook her seat on the swing but Cal did not sit. The fingers of his right hand curled possessively around her neck and she shivered in spite of the warmth from his hand. Staring up at Cal, she smiled and covered his fingers with her own.

"I'm going to check on Drew," Cal said, tactfully dismissing himself.

Lauren nodded, feeling somewhat bereft after he had removed his hand. Her dark gaze followed his retreat as he walked down the steps and disappeared from view.

"Is he back to stay?"

Her gaze swung back to Andrew's, and for the first time since Lauren had known Andrew his eyes were not bright with laughter. The green orbs resembled cold, hard, uncut frosted emeralds.

She felt a prickle of annoyance. What she had felt in the restaurant when she introduced Cal to Andrew had not been her imagination. The two men did not like each other.

"And what's that supposed to mean, Andrew?"

Andrew crossed an ankle over a knee, running his thumb and forefinger down the crease in his tan slacks. His head came up slowly and he impaled her with his angry glare.

"I won't mince words, Lauren."

"Then don't," she retorted stiffly.

"He's going to hurt you."

Lauren smiled a sad smile. "He can't hurt me."

"And why not?"

She inhaled deeply, then let out her breath in a soft shudder. "Because I don't love him," she lied smoothly. "I've never loved him," she added.

Andrew steepled his fingers, bringing them to his mouth. "I don't believe you, Lauren. You married the man, had his child and you don't feel anything for him?"

Lauren tilted her chin in a defiant gesture. "I don't believe you drove out here to discuss Caleb Samuels. Or did you?"

Andrew studied Lauren for a long moment. She looked the same yet something about her was different.

His familiar smile was back in place. "You're right. I didn't. The movie right to option Lloyd Caldwell's book on the Negro baseball leagues has been finalized. Filming is scheduled to begin in Vancouver in two weeks. Caldwell wants you as the technical advisor for the film. The entire project should take about six months. Two to three to shoot and another two to go through production and editing."

The shock of Andrew's disclosure hit Lauren full force. The excitement of working on a movie set paled quickly when she remembered the turn her life had taken—the change based on her decision to remarry Caleb Samuels.

"I can't do it." Her refusal was quiet and final.

Andrew gritted his teeth. "Why not?" he hissed.

"I'm registering Drew for preschool."

"Get him a tutor," Andrew insisted.

Lauren gave him a level look. "Drew needs children his own age, not a tutor."

Bracing his elbows on his knees, Andrew leaned forward. "It's not only Drew, is it?" His voice was soft and coaxing.

She arched an eyebrow and smiled. Very few things escaped Andrew Monroe's quick mind. "I'm getting married."

Andrew arched his own golden eyebrows. "You're going to remarry a man you don't love?"

"I'm doing it for Drew."

"And what does Lauren Taylor expect from this marriage to her son's father?"

"Nothing, Andrew. Nothing."

"You deserve more than nothing, Lauren. You deserve love, trust and fidelity. And judging from what I've read about C. B. Samuels you can't expect . . ." His voice faded when he noted her expression. He had overstepped the boundaries of their friendship.

Andrew was right and Lauren knew it. Both of them knew it. She did not deserve to be hurt a second time. But if she was careful there would be no hurt, no pain. As long as she did not lose her heart to Cal she would be successful and a winner.

"I'm sorry about the film, Andrew."

Andrew sat back on the love seat, shrugging wide shoulders. "It's all right. I'd hoped that you would consider getting into film work."

"Maybe in the future when Drew's older."

Andrew appeared deep in thought as he steepled his fingers. "You're the best researcher I've ever agented."

"That's because I'm the only researcher you've ever agented," Lauren teased.

Andrew's low laugh dispelled the somber mood. "You're right about that. When's the big day?"

"Late July or early August."

"Aren't you rushing it?"

Lauren shook her head. She and Cal had to marry before August twentieth or Drew would forfeit his inheritance to Jacqueline Samuels.

"Am I invited?"

Lauren moved over to the love seat and looped her arm around Andrew's waist. "Of course you are."

Andrew cradled her cheek against his shoulder, pressing his lips to her curling hair. "You've broken my heart, Lauren Taylor."

Pulling back, Lauren glanced up at his crestfallen expression. "If I didn't know you so well I'd believe you, Andrew Monroe."

"You're special to me, Lauren. Very special."

Lauren sobered, seeing his green eyes darken with an unnamed emotion. She and Andrew were a good team. He agented nonfiction authors and the research she compiled for them added to the authenticity of their work.

"And you're very special to me," she replied. "Would you like to see the latest additions to the Taylor menagerie?" Lauren hoped to lighten the mood with talk of Missy's puppies.

Andrew stood, pulling her up with him. "Well, since I can't convince you to marry me and have my children I suppose I'll have to settle with being godfather to your children and providing a home for the offspring of your pets."

She glanced up at Andrew. "You never asked me to marry you."

Andrew followed Lauren into the house. "I was going to, Lauren Taylor."

"Liar," she threw over her shoulder.

"I'm not lying," he protested, staring at the smooth flesh of her bared shoulders and back.

"I would never marry my boss."

Andrew caught up with Lauren in the kitchen. "You're right about that. Because I would never fire you."

Turning, Lauren gave him a long, penetrating look. "Wish me luck, Andrew. I need you to be happy for me."

He leaned closer. "I'll always be happy for you. You deserve the best that life has to offer."

Winding her arms around his waist, she rested her head on his chest. "Thank you, Andrew. Thank you."

* * *

Cal stood in the doorway leading from the garage, watching the intimate interchange between Lauren and Andrew. He managed to quell the rage racing headlong throughout his body. Rage and jealousy. He wanted from Lauren what she so freely offered Andrew Monroe, and at that moment he wanted Lauren. He didn't just want to give her his name again, but all he could offer a woman: his protection, his love and his passion.

Shock after shock rocked him to the core with the rush of possessive waves taunting him.

She's mine, he thought. Lauren was his woman and he wouldn't share her—not with Andrew Monroe and not with any man.

Lauren extracted herself from Andrew's loose embrace and discovered Cal staring at her. He had been so quiet she thought she and Andrew were alone in the kitchen.

But that was something she was beginning to notice about Cal. He entered a room so quietly that when she glanced up he usually startled her with his presence.

Yet his presence was anything but quiet. It screamed and radiated his virility and his brilliance.

"Andrew is going to see the puppies," she explained in an even tone.

Cal nodded and stepped aside. He waited until Andrew disappeared into the garage with Drew and Tommy, then moved toward Lauren.

"I will not put up with my wife being pawed by another man." His voice was like velvet while his eyes flashed fire.

Lauren felt her temper rise. "I'm not your wife."

"You were before and you'll be again."

"Then don't accuse me of anything until I do become your wife again."

Cal captured her upper arms, his thumbs moving sensuously over her bared flesh. "You like him touching you?"

"Stop it, Caleb."

He pulled her closer to his body. "You like him kissing you?"

She couldn't respond as his head came down and he covered her mouth with his. His fingers were like manacles of steel while his lips stroked hers like heated honey. Her fists against his chest eased and unclenched, fingers spreading out and moving up to his broad shoulders.

His tongue swept over her lips, questing and seeking entrance to the moist heat of her mouth. Moaning, she inhaled and her lips parted, giving him the access he sought.

Cal tasted her lips, her tongue, the ridge of her teeth, then the ridged roof of her mouth. The little sounds coming from Lauren made him tremble with desire.

All of his senses were heightened from the crush of her firm breasts against his chest, the heat of her body, the silken feel of her skin and the floral fragrance clinging to her hair and flesh.

Holding her, tasting her—now he knew why he had taken Lauren Taylor to his bed and married her. In her innocence and naïveté, she held nothing back. She was passion, a fire burning out of control.

His hands moved frantically over her back and slid down to her hips. A tortured groan filled the kitchen and it was several seconds before Cal realized it had been his.

He pressed her hips to his middle, permitting her to feel what he was unable to control. His maleness searched through layers of fabric, making her more than aware of his hardness.

Lauren felt as if she were drowning; she was drowning and she didn't want to be rescued. Feelings she had tried to repress surfaced like an explosion, scorching her with fire. The fullness in her breasts spread lower, bringing with it a throbbing dampness.

"Caleb," she moaned, throwing back her head and baring her neck. "Ah-h, Caleb."

He heard his name through the haze of desire and

buried his face in her throat. Gulping for much-needed air, he closed his eyes, trying to regain a measure of control.

His pulses slowed, the ache in his groin eased and he pulled back. What he saw in the depths of Lauren's jet-black eyes shocked him. She wasn't afraid of him. She wanted him. A slight smile softened his mouth.

Registering his smile, Lauren squared her shoulders and tilted her chin. "I suggest you try to exercise more self-control, Caleb Samuels."

"I don't have the willpower, darling," Cal drawled, grinning.

He released her and Lauren turned her back. She wasn't reprimanding Cal but herself. She should've resisted him. She was hopelessly and completely helpless when it came to Caleb Samuels. It was as if her reason for being born female was to exist solely for this man.

Cal took a step, leaning forward and pressing a kiss to the back of her neck. "I'll see you tomorrow," he said softly.

This time when Caleb Samuels left Lauren's house he was grinning broadly. It all had come together. He was one step closer to making Lauren his—forever.

Chapter Nine

Lauren did not know why, but she missed not sharing breakfast with Cal. He had called to inform her that he had an early morning meeting with John Evans to draw up his will, and as she replaced the receiver on its cradle she felt numbed. It was about to begin. Her life was going to change—forever.

After feeding Drew, she sat down with a calendar selecting alternative dates for her wedding.

She decided on a number she needed for invitations, doubling the number in case Cal wanted to invite his relatives and friends.

Lauren also made a note to call Gwen so that they could go and look at dresses. Thinking of Gwen made her wonder how much information she had uncovered on Jacqueline Samuels, and even though Cal had warned her about Jacqueline, Lauren could not bring herself to believe his stepmother would try to sabotage their marriage.

Odessa arrived in time to join Lauren and Drew for lunch. She kissed her grandson with a loud flourish, whispering in his ear the plans she made for their time together.

"Have you set the date?" she asked Lauren, slipping onto the bench beside Drew.

Lauren sat down and passed her mother a bowl of shrimp salad. "The first Saturday in August. That'll give us an extra week."

Odessa nodded. "Have you called Reverend Lewis?"

Lauren paused, shaking her head. "I'm not having a religious ceremony." She watched the natural color drain from Odessa's face, the sprinkling of freckles across her nose and cheeks standing out in vivid contrast.

"Why not, Lauren?"

She bit down hard on her lower lip, inhaling. "I can't be a hypocrite, Mama. I can't get married in church, knowing it's not for the right reasons."

Odessa recovered, taking a sip of lemonade. "What are you planning to do?" Her voice was a raspy whisper.

"Have Uncle Odell marry us at your house."

"Is that what you really want?"

"Yes, Mama. That's what I want."

"What about Caleb? Do you think he'll go along with what you propose?"

Lauren smiled at her mother. "I don't think he'll object."

Not only did Cal object to her decision not to marry in a church, but he was extremely vocal in his objection. He paced the length of the porch, clenched fists thrust in the pockets of his trousers.

"You're selfish, Lauren." He stopped long enough to glare at her. "Not only are you selfish, but you're also spoiled beyond belief.

"How can you raise a child when you're acting like a child?" he continued, not giving Lauren an opportunity to defend herself. "Why is it so difficult for you to compromise?"

Lauren smiled, the gesture further incensing him. She had revealed that she wanted a civil ceremony at her parents' home with her mother's brother, a state supreme court justice, officiating.

"Are you finished, Caleb?" she asked in a saccharine tone.

Cal barely nodded. He was angry enough to shake Lauren until she was too weak to fight him, and she had been fighting him as much as he was fighting his own feelings for her.

He never thought she would get under his skin like an invisible itch, shattering the shield he had put up to resist her. She had wounded him once; it would not happen again.

Lauren rose from the porch swing and moved over to stand in front of Cal, fighting tension as well as frustration.

"Don't talk to me about compromise, Caleb." Her voice was low and calm despite her rising anger. "For the past week I've compromised my life, my very existence. And if your grandfather had died a week later, we would not be having this conversation right now."

His eyes narrowed. "What are you talking about?"

"Andrew came here yesterday to offer me an opportunity to work as a technical advisor on a film about the Negro baseball leagues. I spent more than six months researching the facts for Lloyd Caldwell, feeling what those talented men felt when they walked out on the playing fields in those dusty, hot towns and cities throughout the country. I lived and breathed through the lives of the players, on and off the baseball diamond, knowing many of them prayed every night that they would eventually make it to the major leagues despite the color of their skin. I wanted more than anything else to relive that experience on a movie set.

"I wanted it, Caleb. I wanted it almost as much as I wanted my baby." Turning her back, she closed her eyes. She had not planned to tell Cal about Andrew's offer but it was out and she couldn't retract it.

"I had to turn it down, Caleb, because the next year of

my life doesn't belong to me. It belongs to you and Drew so how selfish can I be?"

Cal walked over to Lauren, his hands going to her shoulders. He encountered his own personal anguish as he noted her pain-filled gaze.

Neither of them would come out of their marriage of convenience unscathed. Lauren would give up her independence for a year while he was willing to give her a lifetime of trying to right the wrongs, unaware that all he wanted from her was love. An emotion that could not be bought or bartered.

"Darling." His voice was low and quiet.

Lauren jerked out of his embrace, taking a backward step; she couldn't stand for him to touch her—not now; not when she hated herself for loving this man as much as she did.

Why couldn't she forget the week on Cay Verde? Why couldn't her mind erase the feel of his hands, the taste of his mouth, the way her body responded to his. How could this man, a stranger, know her better than she knew herself?

She walked with stiff dignity down the porch and around to the back of the house. She wanted to run, but where could she run to escape Cal? Even if she had crossed an ocean he still would continue to haunt her; haunt her like he'd been doing for years.

Lauren flopped down on the colorful hammock strung between two sturdy maple trees. With one leg trailing out of the hammock, she swayed gently in a slow, hypnotic motion.

Closing her eyes, she wondered how her life could change so abruptly. Whenever Caleb Samuels appeared, her world tilted on its axis, not permitting her a modicum of control.

Pulling her leg up into the hammock, she listened to the sounds floating around her. The few moments of solitude she'd managed to capture in the past when she lay in the hammock would become a memory. Cal, who had been a part of her past was now her present and her future.

The crush of a solid male body startled Lauren, and her eyes opened. "What are you doing?" she gasped. Cal quietly and unexpectedly had joined her on the hammock. Either he had to make some noise when he approached or she was certain to experience cardiac arrest.

There wasn't enough room for them to lie side-by-side in the hammock, so Cal shifted and settled her over his body, her breasts flattened against his hard chest and her legs cradled between his.

Lauren's heart pounded wildly as she tried escaping the arm of steel around her waist. "Let me go, Cal."

He lowered his chin and veiled his face in her thick black curled hair. "I can't do that, Lauren." He tightened his hold on her body. "I let you go a long time ago. That will not happen again."

Lauren decided on another plan of defense. "This hammock is going to fall. It's not designed to hold our weight."

Cal smiled, closing his eyes. He did not want to move. The feel of Lauren's body was much too pleasurable.

"We're not overweight, Lauren. It'll hold at least three hundred pounds," he added confidently.

She buried her face in his throat. There was no way she could ignore the swelling hardness pressing intimately against her bare thighs not covered by her shorts.

"Please, Caleb." Now her voice was a throaty whisper.

Cal's hands cupped her hips, holding her captive to his rising desire.

"Please what, *querida?*" he crooned. "Please don't let me go? Or please love me?"

"Please," she repeated weakly.

"I haven't come to you a stranger, Lauren," Cal continued hotly against her ear. "And I haven't come to break up your home and harm our child. I've come to be your husband and your lover." He felt her stiffen. "And

I do want to be your lover," he confirmed in a tone filled with quiet conviction.

"You want free sex, Cal," she said against his chest.

He went rigid. "I don't need 'free sex' as you call it, Lauren. Sex is not the same as desire."

"It is to me," Lauren countered.

"I must teach you the difference," he said, laughing.

"I don't want to learn."

"I know you'd be a quick study, *querida.*"

Lauren tried freeing herself from his embrace and failed. He was too strong.

"Stop wiggling, *querida,* before we fall."

"Stop calling me that."

"What? Darling? But you are my darling," Cal crooned.

Lauren lay still, then when Cal relaxed his grip on her body she scrambled from the hammock. Cal, reaching out, grabbed her shirt and they tumbled heavily to the ground.

Cal cradled her body when they landed, his taking the full force of the fall and all of Lauren's weight.

Lauren gritted her teeth against the shock. Cal's arms fell away and she rolled off his prone form. It took a few seconds to note he hadn't moved.

She felt a rush of blood in her head as she crawled back to Cal. His head rested at a grotesque angle as a sensation of dread washed over her. He was so quiet, so still.

Trembling fingers touched his jaw. Lauren was too upset to register the length of his lashes as they lay on sculpted cheekbones or the exquisite outline of his sensual mouth. She stared at him, feeling the icy fingers of fear replace the heat in her body.

Her fingers trailed down to his neck and she discovered a strongly beating pulse. Lauren whispered a prayer of thanks. He was alive, even though she wasn't certain whether he was conscious.

"Caleb," she said close to his mouth. "Caleb, can you

hear me?" Her slender hands cradled his face. "Please, Caleb . . ." Her voice broke.

"I can't lose you a second time," she continued, trying to gather enough courage to leave him to call for emergency medical assistance.

She felt him shudder, then draw in a deep breath. "Come on, darling," she coaxed softly. "Wake up. Please wake up." Cal moaned, but did not open his eyes. "Don't try to move. I'm going for help." He moaned again. "It's all right, love. I'll be right back." Leaning over, Lauren pressed a tender kiss to his lips.

In less than a heartbeat Lauren found herself on the ground, Cal pressing her down to the thick carpet of grass. His golden eyes impaled her.

"Darling—love," he drawled, leering at her expression of surprise. "I don't want to lose you a second time," he taunted.

Lauren shook with impotent rage as Cal made her his prisoner. "You . . . you low-life. You liar!" she screamed in his face.

Cal settled his full weight on her slight frame. "Liar," he rasped against her moist face. "You're the liar, Lauren Samuels. You're lying to yourself and you've been lying to me."

"I hate you, Caleb," she snapped, as much from anger as from humiliation.

He lowered his head. "No you don't, darling. No more than I can hate you."

Lauren glanced away from the golden orbs that probed beneath the surface to see what she had vainly tried to conceal.

"You can't hide, darling, no more than I can continue to lie to you or myself," Cal continued. Her lids fluttered then came up and he smiled a tender smile. "I want to make love to you."

Lauren buried her forehead against his shoulder. How could she tell him that she would give herself to him, there on the grass at that moment, if only he told her that he loved her? That she would offer him all she could as his former and future wife.

Cal shifted and reversed their positions, holding her protectively. "If I could, I would put you inside of me, Lauren. I need you just that much."

She registered his words and her heart wept. Cal had openly shown her his vulnerability for the first time. He was hurting and she was watching him bleed.

Winding her arms around his neck, she breathed deeply against his throat. "We'll make it, Cal," she said quietly.

He smiled, burying his face in her hair. He was certain they would make it. They would make it because Lauren possessed what he had sought all of his life. To him she embodied a family unit: mother, father, child and home, and becoming a part of a family unit was as precious to him as taking his next breath.

"Are we going out tonight?" he questioned softly.

"I have to think about going out with you," she replied.

Pulling back, Cal stared down at her impassive face, unable to conceal his disappointment. "Why?"

Lauren felt her stomach muscles tighten. Cal looked so much like Drew did whenever she turned down the child's request to do something he truly wanted to do.

"Because you gave me a wicked scare, Caleb Samuels."

Cal's gaze drank up her beautiful delicate features. Cradling her face between his hands, he leaned over and touched her mouth with his. "I'll never do that again, darling. Never," he promised, taking full possession of her sweet, hot mouth.

Lauren gave herself up to the magic of the man and the moment; a man she loved; a man she would love as long as she lived.

* * *

Cal waited for Lauren to change clothes before suggesting they return to Boston where he could also change. Their unexpected romp on the grass had left noticeable stains on his pristine white shirt, and it was after five o'clock by the time he maneuvered his Porsche into a spacious parking lot along the waterfront area in Newburyport.

Historic Newburyport's downtown area, a National Historic Landmark, had been remodeled in its original Federalist style. Newburyport was Lauren's favorite city in the Commonwealth of Massachusetts.

Lauren walked alongside Cal, a light breeze lifting the flap of a hip-fitting cotton sarong-style skirt in an orange and black jungle print over her smooth, shapely legs while the warm summer sun beat down on her exposed arms under a bright orange silk tank top. A pair of black patent-leather slip-on sandals completed her winning, attractive attire.

"Slow down, Cal," she protested, trying to keep pace with his leisurely long-legged stride.

He tucked her hand into the bend of his elbow, slowing his pace. "I'm sorry," he apologized, smiling down at her.

Lauren felt her breath catch in her throat as she returned his smile. Caleb Samuels was breathtakingly attractive in his cambric shirt and slacks. The thin white linen fabric was a startling contrast against his deeply tanned golden-brown skin.

"Are you hungry?" he asked, taking furtive glances at her soft passionate mouth.

"A little. Do you mind if I suggest the restaurant?"

"Of course not."

Cal was pleased when Lauren said that the restaurant served excellent food while catering to casual dining and attire, for he wanted to relive the casual, relaxed atmosphere they had experienced during their stay on Cay Verde.

However, in contrast to the solitude of Cay Verde, the

narrow streets of Newburyport were crowded with pedestrians. Tourists, with cameras hanging from necks and shoulders, stopped to peer into windows at every novelty shop and Lauren was as amused at Cal when he lingered on the boardwalk along the Waterfront Park and Promenade to watch the boats bobbing weightlessly on the Merrimack River. It was with much reluctance that he left and she steered him in the direction of The Grog.

The sounds of live music and laughter greeted their entrance. It was the dinner hour and the restaurant was alive with tantalizing smells and high spirits.

They were shown a table after a short wait and given menus. The smiling young waitress gave Cal an eyeful of thick fluttering lashes and straight sparkling teeth.

"Would you like a cocktail?" she asked, addressing Cal.

He arched an eyebrow at Lauren. She nodded. "Please give us a moment to decide."

The waitress did not move. She continued to stare at Cal. "Aren't you C. B. Samuels?" she questioned in a nervous, breathless twitter. "My father has all of your books," she continued in the same twittering tone. "Wait until I tell him that I served you," she gushed.

Lauren smiled at Cal's bemused expression after the young woman finally walked away. He hadn't confirmed or denied that he was C. B. Samuels.

"Your public hasn't forgotten you, C.B.," she teased.

Cal grimaced. "Very funny, Lauren." He took a glance at the menu, his burnished-gold eyes moving slowly over the printed words. "What do you say we share a bottle of champagne?"

Lauren thought about the two glasses of champagne she had shared with Gwen. Resting her chin on the heel of her hand, she gave him a sensual smile. "What are we celebrating?"

His gaze met hers, his eyes crinkling in laughter. "Why, our engagement, of course."

"Okay." Her voice, dropping an octave, contained a

breathless quality. She was caught in a snare of Cal's making, unable to free herself from his powerful, magical aura. She noted the attractive cleft in his chin and the sensual curve of his full upper lip. She surveyed his face, committing it to memory, for she would need the memories—all of them—after their year of marriage ended.

"What would you like to eat?" Cal reluctantly pulled his gaze away from her beautiful face.

Lauren knew what she wanted, without looking at the menu. "I'd like a cup of clam chowder and the chicken fajitas."

Cal perused the menu further, then signaled the staring waitress, giving her their order.

Over glasses of champagne, chowder and their entrées, Lauren and Cal discussed the plans for their upcoming wedding. Cal agreed on the first Saturday in August, promising he would call his mother so she could reserve her flight from Barcelona.

"Is there anyone else you'd like to invite?" she asked him. "Cousins, uncles or aunts?"

He shook his head. "You, Drew and my mother are all the family that I claim."

She was curious about whether he actually had other relatives, but decided against asking. "Will it bother you if we don't get married in a church?"

Again Cal shook his head, his eyes fixed on her face. "No, Lauren, I don't mind."

"Where are we going for our honeymoon?" He had conceded to a civil ceremony, and it was only fair that she concede to a honeymoon.

"To the Berkshires," Cal replied with a wide grin.

"I'm not much for roughing it, Caleb," she retorted.

"It's quite civilized, love. The house has indoor plumbing and electricity."

She studied his smirking expression. "Is it your house?"

"Yes. I bought it after the sale of my first book," he admitted. "I use it for a writing retreat."

Lauren swirled a small amount of the pale bubbling wine around in her glass, staring at the gold liquid. "When was the last time you used it?"

Cal stared down at his outstretched fingers on the tabletop. The overhead light glinted off the signet ring on his left hand. "About three months ago."

Lauren felt her heart leap. She had no idea Cal had been in the States. "How often had you come to the States?"

"Two, maybe three times a year." His gaze caught and held hers. "And my grandfather never once hinted that I had fathered a child."

Lauren shook her head in amazement. "Dr. Samuels knew the living couldn't argue with the dead, so he waited to die to become the master puppeteer, pulling the strings and manipulating lives."

"He was quite a character," Cal stated, smiling.

"I have a feeling you like all of this."

Cal's eyes roved leisurely over her face and down to her revealing neckline. His gaze and laugh was lecherous.

"I couldn't have thought of a better plot if my life depended on it," he confessed.

Lauren managed to look insulted. "You have a dirty laugh, Caleb."

That's not all that's dirty, Cal thought. His mind conjured up the sensual image of Lauren naked—hot and moaning in his arms.

"There's nothing dirty about what I want to do with you," he stated solemnly.

Lauren sobered when she saw the liquid fire ignite the golden flames in his eyes. Her insides swirled, skidded, her body warming and growing heavy. The heat in her face flamed under his entrancing examination. Her hand shook slightly as she raised her glass to her lips and swallowed the dry, bubbling wine.

"It's going to happen, Lauren, whether we want it or not," he predicted.

The invisible web of attraction that had been so apparent years before was stronger, nearly out of control. Lauren's mind told her to resist, but her body refused to follow the dictates of her brain.

"Sleeping together will change everything," she said.

"It will only change us," Cal argued softly.

That was what Lauren feared; she didn't want to change; she wanted to hold onto the memory of Caleb Samuels without experiencing the pain of losing him twice.

She straightened in her chair, pulling her shoulders back. The motion stretched the silk fabric of her top taut over her breasts, drawing Cal's fevered gaze to the firm mounds of flesh. She hadn't worn a bra under the bright orange garment.

Cal closed his eyes, still seeing the outline of her nipples thrusting against the silk top. More images came rushing back. He remembered Lauren's breasts. They were small and firm, with disproportionately large dark nipples. Even before he had tasted her breasts the nipples were hard and distended. Fire shot through his groin and he groaned.

Lauren peered closely at Cal. "Are you all right?"

No, he wanted to scream. He wasn't all right. He was in pain; a hot, throbbing, excruciating pain that could only be relieved by her.

"I'm fine," he lied, opening his eyes. He hated lying to her, but how could he tell Lauren that he hurt and that his pain was emotional and physical.

"Do you want dessert?" he asked through clenched teeth.

"No, darling," she crooned.

Cal shifted uncomfortably, knowing he couldn't stand up without Lauren noting his arousal. "I think I'll have something," he said quickly. Sitting and eating would give him the time needed to bring his raw passions under control.

Half an hour later Lauren and Cal walked out of The

Grog and onto Middle Street. His large hand closed possessively over her fingers, pulling her to his side.

"I think we need to walk off a few calories," she suggested. They had shared the generous slice of apple pie à la mode.

"Where do you want to go?"

"Market Square. There's a sweetshop that sells homemade fudge and assorted truffles that my mother can't resist."

Cal followed Lauren's lead, his arm going around her waist. "Your mother isn't the only one who can't resist candy. There're times when I have an uncontrollable craving for something sweet."

Lauren's right arm curved around his slim solid body. "I thought you were more controlled than that," she teased.

"There are certain passions I never want to control," he countered, kissing her ear.

She had no problem interpreting his double meaning, knowing what particular passion he was referring to. Making love to Cal conjured up unbidden memories and the blood roared hotly in her face and body.

They turned down Market Square and Cal stopped in front of a jewelry shop. The showcase displayed a large selection of antique pieces.

"You need a ring, Lauren," he stated, then steered her into the beautifully appointed shop.

A woman with short gleaming silver hair and a rich gold tan smiled at Cal. "May I help you with something?"

"I need an engagement ring for my fiancée and bands for both of us."

Lauren was too surprised to respond until the salesclerk reached for her left hand to measure her third finger.

"Caleb," she warned quietly, but a scowl from him preempted any further protest.

"A five," the woman murmured. "You have very slim

fingers." She glanced down into the display case. "What's your preference? Antique? Contemporary?"

"Contemporary."

"Antique."

Cal and Lauren had spoken in unison.

"Antique," Lauren insisted, giving Cal the *look*.

"I think I have something you'd like," the woman said, reaching into the case for a ring with a large oval diamond.

Lauren shook her head. "Not that one." If she was going to have an engagement ring she wanted one that suited her personal taste. "I'd like to try that one."

Cal leaned closer, his chest pressing against her back. A slow smile parted his lips. Lauren had chosen one with an exquisite emerald-cut diamond, flanked by square-cut baguettes.

"I like it," he stated. Taking the ring from the woman's hand, he slipped it onto Lauren's finger. It fit perfectly. "It was made for you, darling." His voice was as soft and soothing as a caress.

Lauren held her hand out in front of her, her heart pounding uncontrollably. The ring was magnificent.

"Do you want it?" Cal questioned, smiling at her dazed expression.

"Yes." The single word was barely audible.

The salesclerk smiled at the young entranced couple. She touched Cal's hand to garner his attention. "I'd like to measure your finger to fit you for a band. I suppose you'd want matching bands?"

"Yes," Lauren and Cal chorused.

It took longer to select bands which suited both of their tastes. They finally decided on an unadorned style that was in keeping with the elegant simplicity of Lauren's engagement ring.

Cal extracted a credit card from his wallet and gave it to the salesclerk. His expression did not change as he signed for the purchase. Lauren was worth every penny he would ever spend on her, for she represented something money could not buy. She was his security, his ultimate success.

"Thank you, Cal," Lauren said softly, giving him a demure smile, "for the ring and the bracelet."

His face creased into a sudden smile. "Oh, so you did find the bracelet?"

She basked in the shared moment of their bliss. "Yes, and I intend to wear it on special occasions like weddings, birthdays, graduations and for the birth of our many grandchildren," she stated, repeating the toast he had made the week before.

You forgot *our* children, Cal thought, for he knew as surely as his encompassing love for Lauren that she would bear another child—his child.

They made their way across the street and into Something Sweet and purchased an assortment of fudge, brittle and truffles for Odessa. Lauren beamed with pride when a saleswoman complimented her on her ring. She thanked the woman and looped her arm through Cal's as they left the shop.

So this is the way it feels to be promised to someone, she mused. She had to admit it was comforting and gave her a sense of protection.

Lauren then realized that Cal wanted all of the traditions that went along with a man and woman planning a life together—engagement, rings and wedding ceremony, and she wondered if he was being traditional because of his parents' unorthodox marriages.

I'll make it work, she thought, her fingers biting into the flesh on Cal's arm. *I'll make him fall in love with me again so he won't leave after the year is over.*

"A nickel for your thoughts, *querida*," he said, watching her expression change.

Lauren stopped and stared up at him. The thick lashes framing her large dark eyes were like a fringe of black velvet. Her mouth softened in a smile. "I feel so wonderfully happy, Cal," she confessed without guile.

He cradled her chin in one hand, his thumb tracing the delicate curve of her jaw. Lauren's sable-brown skin felt like satin to his touch. He had stopped questioning why fate had led him to her, and he opened himself to receive everything she had to offer.

"Making you happy makes me happy, darling." There was a slight hint of wonder in his voice, as if he hadn't expected her to be truthful with him.

But what Cal wanted to hear most from Lauren she withheld. He wanted to hear that she loved him.

"Where do you want to go now, *querida?*"

"Let's go home," she suggested in a low inviting tone.

Cal needed no further prompting. Lauren was feeling what he felt. They wanted to be alone—with each other.

Chapter Ten

Lauren stared through the windshield as Cal maneuvered his sports car into the driveway to her house. She moved her left hand and a shaft of fading sunlight caught the precious stones on her finger. Within a month she was to become Mrs. Caleb Samuels for the second time, and, as before, he was still a stranger—a stranger she had married, a stranger whose child she had borne, and a stranger she loved without question.

She tried weighing all that had culminated since the reading of the late Dr. Caleb Samuels's will. Events occurred so quickly that she found it difficult to sort out what was real and what was not an ongoing dream where she would wake up in a cold sweat.

But this Caleb Samuels was real—a hot, breathing, flesh-and-blood man, and she was also alive. The part of her Lauren thought had died when she walked out on Cal was also alive—hot and breathing, and she wanted nothing more than to lie in Cal's arms and experience again what it meant to be a fulfilled woman.

At that moment Lauren knew she had to stop hiding, running and lying. She wanted Caleb Samuels. There was never a time when she didn't want him.

"I have to see after Missy, then throw a few things in an overnight bag," she said quietly

Cal merely nodded. He did not move as Lauren slipped

out of the car and made her way up the steps to the porch. He sat, shaken, amazed and overwhelmed with the emotions gripping his mind and body. Lauren was ready to come to him willingly, without fear, and offering all that he had sought since he first slept with her.

Lauren checked her answering machine for messages, finding one from her cousin. Gwen had reported that Jacqueline Samuels was in partnership with a record producer specializing in new talent.

Gwen also said that it had been rumored that Jacqueline was instrumental in breaking up her partner's marriage when his wife returned unexpectedly from a business trip and found her husband and Jacqueline in bed together at their vacation bungalow on Martha's Vineyard.

"Nice lady," Lauren mumbled under her breath.

She did not want to think about Jacqueline. She had enough to think about when she realized what was to happen.

Methodically she packed what she needed for her overnight stay at Cal's house, turning and making her way downstairs before she could change her mind.

Lauren found Cal in the garage with Missy and her puppies. The large canine was standing with her front paws on Cal's chest while the two tiny gray pups sniffed at his feet. She smiled, unable to believe Missy could be that playful.

"I changed her water and gave her enough food until we get back tomorrow," Cal said around Missy's shaggy head. He pushed her gently until she regained her footing.

Missy ambled toward Lauren, sniffing her cautiously. She held out a tentative hand, patting her pet. "Take care of your babies, little mother." Missy responded with a loud bark.

Cal took Lauren's tapestry overnight bag from her

loose grip. He smiled at her and she returned it, success-fully masking the glint of uneasiness in her eyes.

"Let's go, *querida.*"

Lauren wasn't able to draw a normal breath until Cal parked the racy sports car in front of the town house that had belonged to four generations of Samuelses.

"I hope you don't drive that fast with Drew," she admonished with a frown. Cal smiled sheepishly, giving her a sidelong glance. "Caleb, no," Lauren wailed.

His right hand caught the back of her head—incredibly strong fingers holding her captive. "I'm careful, sweet-heart."

Lauren pounded his chest with a small fist. "Don't you dare sweetheart me, Caleb Samuels. Careful isn't enough. If you hurt my child I'll . . ."

Cal caught her hand in an iron grip. "Drew is also my child, Lauren." He thrust his face close to hers. "You have to stop thinking of him as *your* child. He's *ours.*"

She rested her forehead on his shoulder, closing her eyes and inhaling his distinctive masculine scent.

"I know he's ours. It's just that he's been mine for so long."

Cal smiled in the shadowy darkness of the car. Drew was his and Lauren was his. Curving a hand under her chin, he lowered his head, brushing his lips over hers.

"Let's not fight, Lauren." She nodded. "Are you ready to go in?" She nodded again.

Lauren undid her seat belt while Cal climbed out of the car and came around to help her out. He picked up her overnight bag and the decorative shopping bag with Odessa's fudge and truffles.

Cal felt Lauren hesitate as he took her arm to lead her into the town house. "What's the matter, darling?"

She stared up at the building's facade. "I was just remembering the first time I came here with you. I was so frightened. And I'll never forget the way your grandfather glared at me. He hated me, Cal."

Cal tightened his grip. "No, he didn't, Lauren. He was more angry with me than he could've ever been with you. He claimed I gave you up too easily."

"I didn't leave you a choice."

A cold, hard expression settled across his features. "But I did have a choice, Lauren. I could've refused to let you go. I could've fought you and not agreed to the annulment. But I didn't because I saw what it did to Mother when she wanted out of her marriage. She cried that she felt trapped and there were times she was so depressed that I feared for her sanity.

"So I didn't fight you because I wanted you happy, darling. That's all I've ever wanted for you, and that was for you to be happy with me."

Lauren offered him a small, shy smile. "But I am happy with you, Cal."

His dark expression did not change. "But you weren't..."

She cut his words off by placing her fingers over his mouth. "I am now, *querido.*"

Her attempt to speak Spanish amused Cal as the corners of his mouth tilted in laughter. "What other words do you know?"

"All of the curses," Lauren confessed, laughing.

He laughed harder. "You would."

They were still laughing when they walked into the living room. Cal sobered and he watched Lauren's reaction as she visually examined her surroundings. He hadn't known she was apprehensive about coming to the place that had been home to a countless number of Samuelses. There was so much he did not know about Lauren Taylor, and there was so much he wanted to know about her and it bothered him that he had only known her physically.

"What would you like, Lauren? What do you want me to give you?" he asked in a quiet voice.

Lauren, surprised by his request, wanted to say, *your love*, but said instead, "Just you, Caleb Samuels. Just you."

Cal pulled her close, holding her gently, protectively. "You have me, baby. All of me."

She wound her arms around his waist, pressing her cheek to his chest. Tears of joy filled her eyes and she blinked them back before they fell. "Thank you, Caleb."

A deep chuckle filled his chest. "If I'd known that all you wanted was me, then I could've saved a few dollars by not going into jewelry stores." He caught her right hand, placing light kisses on her fingers when he felt them curled into a fist. "Just teasing, love. You're worth every penny I'll ever spend on you."

Lauren pulled back and smiled up him. "I'd better call my mother and let her know where I am."

She walked over to the telephone, and dialed her parents' number. Odessa answered after the second ring. "Hi, Mama. I just wanted to call and let you know where to find me if something comes up."

"What on earth can come up, Lauren Vernice Taylor? And if it did, don't you think I'd know where to find you," Odessa grumbled.

Lauren watched Cal watching her and she turned her back. "Mama, I'm not at home," she continued softly. "I'm here in Boston—at Cal's house."

There was a stark, pregnant silence. "You . . . you're spending the night with . . . Caleb?" Odessa's voice had dropped to a whisper.

"Yes, I'm spending the night with Caleb," Lauren replied firmly, and without giving Odessa an opportunity to say anything else, she read off the number on the telephone. "Cal and I will pick Drew up after breakfast."

"Make it after dinner," Odessa shot back. "It appears that you're going to be busy and so am I. My grandson and I have plans to take in a matinee. We also have a few other things to do before dinner."

"Mother!"

"Good night, Lauren. Now you and Caleb have fun."

Lauren held the receiver to her ear, listening to a droning dial tone. She replaced the receiver, shaking her head.

"What did she say?" Cal had noted her blank expression.

"She said we can't pick Drew up until after dinner. They've made plans to do a few things."

Cal came closer to Lauren, a devastatingly irresistible smile parting his lips. "Aside from her beauty, I knew there was something about your mother I couldn't resist."

Lauren took a step backwards. "What's that?" Her eyes were wide, her breathing shallow.

"Her perception," he said, reaching for her when a wall blocked further retreat.

"Caleb!" Lauren whispered in desperation.

"Too late," Cal countered. "You're my captive for the next twenty-four hours, darling. Screaming, begging or praying won't help."

"No, please . . ." The rest was lost as Cal swept her up in his arms, kissing her deeply. Her world spun as he carried her out of the living room and up the stairs to the bedroom where they had slept years ago.

He lowered her gently to his bed, his body following, cradling her with his warmth, strength and masculinity.

Cal rained kisses all over her face and neck, and the small fists pressed against his chest unclenched, then her hands moved sensuously up and down his back. He felt her heat, inhaled her fragrance and tasted the sweet ambrosia of her mouth.

His hands slipped to her waist, pulling her top from the confines of her skirt. He was touching her, tasting her, but Cal wanted to see Lauren—all of her.

Reaching out, he flicked on a bedside lamp, flooding the room with a soft yellow glow.

Lauren closed her eyes and tried to turn over but Cal was too quick. His hands held her captive, and even though she struggled against his loose grip she couldn't free herself. He held her captive—her heart and her body.

Cal rested one arm over Lauren's upraised ones, while his free hand inched her tank top up her midriff over her breasts until he freed her of the silk garment.

She heard his breathing deepen as it exploded from him. Opening her eyes, she stared up into the amber eyes burning her naked breasts.

Cal felt the blood pool in his groin, the swelling hard and heavy between his thighs. Having Lauren like this, in his bed, in his life, was something he had prayed for over and over once he'd lost her; finding her again, possessing her again had unlocked his heart and his soul.

Slowly, painfully, methodically, he rediscovered her body kissing every inch of bared skin he caressed. "Beautiful," Cal whispered reverently. "You are so very beautiful, *querida.*"

Lauren felt beautiful; beautiful, adored and loved. She had made the right decision to share herself with Cal. With him she felt alive, a complete woman.

As Cal placed tiny kisses along the sloping curve of her rib cage, Lauren wound her fingers in his hair, around his ears, then her fingers grazed the smoothness of his clean-shaven jaw.

"Caleb," she gasped as the heat from his mouth seared the junction at her thighs.

Quickly, smoothly, Cal reversed their position, his strong hands cupping the fullness of her bottom. "Don't move, darling. Please, don't move."

His passions were raging out of control and Cal didn't want to spill out his own pleasure before giving Lauren hers.

But Lauren did move as she unbuttoned Cal's shirt, baring his broad chest to her heated gaze, discovering his chest was darker than his face—a deeper, richer tawny brown.

Bending lower, she placed small kisses along the strong column of his throat, then down over the muscles of his smooth chest. Her fingers clutched wide shoulders as she leaned closer, rotating her hips against his.

The heat rising from Cal's skin was clean and masculine and Lauren savored the erotic sensation as her exploration grew bolder. Lowering her head, her tongue flicked over the flat circle of his breast, bringing the nipple to a hard, pebbly beading.

Cal's hands tightened into fists and he struggled valiantly not to toss Lauren onto her back and finish what he had begun.

Closing his eyes, he swallowed back a groan. Her hot mouth went from one breast to the other as Lauren suckled him like a starving infant seeking succor. His groans became strangled gasps and he threw back his head in supplication.

Lauren lay flat on Cal's prone figure, pressing her bare chest to his. She was aware of all of the changes taking place in his body and the unrestrained sounds of sexual pleasure erupting from the back of his throat.

The runaway pounding of his heart filled her with a strange feeling of power. She did excite Cal; she could please him. A hot ache rose within her own body and she prayed she could continue to play out her role as seducer before begging him to take her.

His large hands cradled the back of her head as she kissed him, hard and deep. Deprivation, longings, desires and all of the love Lauren felt for Caleb Samuels poured from her hungry mouth.

He shuddered violently. It was not from passion as much as it was from fear; the fear that Lauren possessed the power to control him—totally. Her hands, her mouth, her body took him beyond himself where he could not recognize the person he had become. She held his present, his future and his very life within her grasp and she did not know it. All he needed from Lauren was a word, a gesture of rejection and he would cease to exist.

Lauren's fingertips feathered over Cal's ribs to the

waistband of his slacks. Her breath was coming faster but she couldn't stop. She had to finish what she had begun.

Rising slightly, her mouth still hungrily devouring her lover's, she unzipped his slacks. The heat from Cal's lower body escaped like tongues of fire from a roaring furnace. Her hands slipped lower, over low-cut briefs, closing on the solid bulge straining for escape.

Cal's control was shattered. "No!" It was too much.

Lauren ignored his protest, gently increasing the pressure and the pleasure on his swollen, throbbing maleness. "Yes, Caleb," she whispered.

"No," he repeated. Quickly reversing their positions and their roles, he held her effortlessly as his captive, his eyes glittering wildly like those of a cornered animal. The muted light from the lamp shadowed his face, but not the brilliant golden eyes with the dark brown centers that stood out like beacons.

Cal shrugged out of his shirt and his raw sensuality sucked Lauren in whole. The muscles rippling in his upper body under skin layered with pigments of ocher and alizarin brown, the film of moisture bathing his flesh and the natural musky male scent of his body and after-shave assaulted all of her senses. Caleb B. Samuels II was beautiful; he was perfect; he was so unequivocally and undeniably male that it screamed out its very essence.

"Thank you, darling," he crooned, having regained control of his runaway passions. Now it was his turn to return the pleasure. He would love Lauren unselfishly as she had loved him.

He removed her skirt, bikini panties and her sandals, stroking her like a master violinist caressing a priceless Stradivarius. He became a sculptor, his fingers moving and lingering over every curve, every plane. "Now it's time I give you something back."

Something in his tone should have warned Lauren, but she was totally unprepared as he slid down the length of the bed and knelt at her feet, moving up and tasting naked flesh in his journey to stake his claim not only on her body but also her heart.

Lauren rediscovered all of her erogenous zones: the soles of her feet, behind her knees, the inside of her thighs and even her armpits.

Cal left a moist trail over the fullness of her buttocks, ignoring her soft pleas that he stop. He had no intention of stopping; not until he loved every sweet, smooth inch of her silken body.

His head dipped between her thighs. "Caleb! Oh, Cal . . ." she cried out, gasping uncontrollably.

Stop, Caleb, her head screamed. Her protests echoed loudly in her brain until her throbbing flesh responded to his methodical ministration.

"I . . ." The rest was lost in the gasps and sobs of ecstasy escaping her constricted throat. She couldn't disguise her body's reaction, arching against his thrusting tongue, her hips undulating in a wild, unrestrained rhythm.

Emotions welled up in Lauren and she did not understand nor could she explain them. Tears formed behind her eyelids and flowed down her cheeks. The pleasure had shattered her into tiny pieces, stripping her bare where she lay naked and vulnerable for the pain only Cal could inflict.

Cal felt her trembling. He also registered her sighs of repletion as he inhaled her feminine muskiness, his tongue catching the droplets clinging to the tangled curls between her silken thighs. He moaned, taking a deep breath.

"You're a joy, darling," he crooned, nibbling at the moist mound. "Beautiful, loving and so wonderful."

He slipped out of his slacks and underwear, then moved over Lauren's limp form. Moisture coated her body, shimmering on her sable skin like dappled sunlight.

She wound her arms around his neck, crying softly. "Shh-h, baby. Don't cry." His touch was gentle, his voice comforting, but Lauren couldn't stop her tears.

He held her until she quieted. She loved him so much

she hurt. She thought she would find love satisfying and peaceful, but she was wrong. Knowing she would lose Cal after a year stabbed at Lauren, making her bleed.

After a long silence, Cal asked, "Are you all right, sweetheart?"

Lauren sniffed loudly. "Yes, Caleb."

He kissed her forehead, brushing back damp curls. "Did I hurt you?"

"No," she answered with a soft laugh.

Cal pulled back and stared down at her spikey wet lashes. "Then, baby, why the tears?"

Lauren buried her face in the hollow between his shoulder and neck. "Because it was so good, so magical," she confessed softly.

"That was only the beginning," he promised, dropping a kiss on the top of her head.

Raising her chin, Lauren stared up at Cal. "Really?"

"Really," he repeated, kissing the end of her nose. He found it hard to believe that Lauren was so womanly, yet at times reacted so innocently. He smiled and she returned his smile, and Cal felt a stirring in his loins. Groaning, he closed his eyes.

Catching her lower lip between her teeth, Lauren inhaled sharply. Cal's hardness searched between her thighs, seeking possession.

"Ah-h," she gasped.

"Oh, yeah," he countered, his lips brushing her as he reached over to the bedside table to secure the foil packets secreted in the drawer.

In less than a minute he was buried deep in her burning body, their breaths mingling and fusing.

Cal moved slowly, deliberately, savoring the moist heat of her tightness. Gritting his teeth, he called on all of his control not to end the exquisite pleasure hurtling through his lower body. He wanted to prolong the poised explosion just a bit longer; long enough to offer Lauren all he had: his love.

Gripping the pillows cradling her head, Cal pulled back, then plunged deeply. He increased his rhythm, and Lauren began moving in concert with him, faster and faster, harder and deeper. A wild, primal cry erupted from the back of his throat and he released the explosive, rushing obsession that had been building, ever since the moment he was reunited with Lauren Taylor.

The first time he had taken Lauren to his bed it had been in lust and passion. This time it was in love and passion.

He loved her; he loved her with everything he had to give another human being.

A quiet, soothing feeling swept over him as his passions ebbed with a comforting pulsing. He had come home. The woman cradled in his arms was his safe harbor.

Fulfilled, they lay together, limbs tangled in exhausted pleasure. Cal shifted and Lauren snuggled against his length. A satisfied smile touched her thoroughly kissed mouth as she fell asleep.

It was later, much later, that Cal joined her in sleep.

Lauren heard the distant ringing through the thick fog of sated slumber. She stretched, her leg encountering an immovable object. She came awake immediately, sitting up.

"Stop wiggling, Lauren," a drowsy male voice ordered.

Turning to her right, she tried making out Cal's face in the darkened bedroom. There was only the sound of his soft breathing.

"Caleb," she whispered loudly.

Cal turned over quickly and flicked on the lamp, his amber gaze encountering her wide stare.

"What is it?" His voice was gruff, but he couldn't help it. It had taken hours before he found solace in the comforting arms of sleep. Making love to Lauren had disturbed him and he knew he could not and would not let her go after the time limit expired on their arranged marriage.

Lauren pulled the edge of the sheet up over her naked breasts. "I thought I heard the phone ringing."

Cal inched closer to Lauren, pulling the sheet out of her grasp, his gaze lingering on her breasts. They were perfect, even though they were small. He reveled in their firmness and the ripe succulence of her large dark nipples.

"You could've come up with a better excuse to wake me if you wanted me to make love to you, *querida,*" he crooned, winking at her.

She felt her face and body heat up under his accusation when Cal pointed to the silent telephone on the bedside table.

"But I did hear the telephone," she insisted. She met his burning golden eyes, her pride surfacing. "If I wanted you to make love to me I'd just come out and say it."

He moved over her body. "Say it," he challenged, his breath hot and searing against her throat.

"No," Lauren retorted, closing her eyes when his fingers inched up her inner thigh.

"Say it," Cal repeated in the heat of her moist mouth, his hand finding her feminine garden of secret pleasures.

She arched against his questing finger, taking all that he offered and countering his challenge with, "If you want me you'll have to take me."

He took her, much like the first time they'd shared a bed. Holding nothing back, they offered each other unbridled, primitive mating.

It ended with Cal bracing his back against the headboard, gasping for breath while Lauren lay trembling from the ecstasy that lingered long after Cal had withdrawn from her body.

Both of them were frightened; frightened as to where their passions would lead and what they would become if they ever parted.

Chapter Eleven

Lauren snapped the ruby and diamond bracelet around her right wrist, fingers lingering over the circle of gold and precious stones. She had promised Cal she would wear his gift for their wedding.

Sucking in her breath, she closed her eyes. Their wedding; she and Caleb Samuels were to become husband and wife for the second time.

Events of the past month had begun like a whirlwind, then escalated. All of the responses were acknowledged from invited guests, the caterers had finalized the menu, she and Cal had picked up their marriage license and Cal had moved most of his clothes and personal items into her house in North Grafton.

Still experiencing the effects of differing time zones, Joelle Samuels helped a frantic Odessa pull together all of the loose ends for their children's wedding.

Opening her eyes, Lauren stared back at her reflection in a full-length mirror. Her wedding attire was not the traditional white lace and satin gown but a floor-length, long-sleeve white satin and Alençon-lace fitted sheath with a side drape and high slit. Beaded pearls banded the low-décolleté oversized collar, sleeves and the seductive scalloped slit and hem, and two large satin roses were nestled along the soft folds of the draped fabric. Her headpiece, a small pillbox hat with a veil of pearl sprays and beading complemented her thoroughly modern dress.

Odessa, Joelle and Gwen stared in silence when Lauren turned to face them. She managed a nervous smile. "I'm ready."

"Caleb has chosen well," Joelle stated proudly in a soft voice that still carried a trace of a Louisiana drawl.

"Thank you," Lauren replied, her smile widening.

Joelle nodded, smiling. Tall, reed-thin and exotic-looking in appearance, fifty-five-year-old Joelle Samuels turned heads everywhere she went.

"You're beautiful, baby," Odessa mumbled, sniffling back tears.

Lauren's hands curled into tight fists. "Oh, Mama, if you start crying I won't be able to walk out of this room."

Gwen Taylor knew if her aunt cried so would Lauren. "Aunt Dessa, please." Her mind churning quickly, she walked to the bedroom door and opened it. "Uncle Roy!"

Roy Taylor rushed into the bedroom, staring at the four women. "What's the matter?" His jet-black eyes shifted frantically over the feminine forms covered in silk and satin.

"Mama's going to start crying," Lauren whispered.

Roy took charge. "Joelle, you take Dessa downstairs while Gwendolyn and I will take care of Laurie." In his own rush of nerves he had reverted back to the name he had called Lauren when she was a child.

Roy placed both hands on his daughter's shoulders and pulled her to his body. "You have to forgive your mother, Laurie. She hasn't been herself lately."

Lauren nodded. No one had been themselves lately. It seemed as if she and Cal managed to argue over nothing and everything. The one time he raised his voice to her she threw a pillow against the wall after he stalked out of the house and drove away.

Tilting her chin, Lauren stared up at her father. "I just want it over, Daddy."

Roy heard his daughter's desperate plea. Lauren had undergone a lot of strain since Caleb Samuels walked back into her life. He kissed her forehead, smiling. "Let's go downstairs and get it over."

Cal stared at Lauren's profile throughout the brief civil ceremony. He was spellbound, unable to pull his gaze away from her face.

She was enchanting. His bride was like a summer rose, slowly opening and coming forth in a full flowering fragrant fragility.

"The ring, Caleb."

Judge Odell Parker's sonorous voice shattered Cal's entrancement with his lovely bride. He extended his hand to Drew and the child slipped the circle of gold off his thumb and placed it in his father's outstretched palm.

Drew, dressed in white short pants, knee socks and shoes, a crisp white shirt with an Eton collar and white tie had the honor of being his father's Best Man. He found it difficult to control his childish excitement as the time neared for his parents' wedding.

Cal slipped the ring on Lauren's finger, grinning proudly.

Lauren repeated the action as she slipped a matching band on Cal's long, tapered finger.

"By the power given me by the Commonwealth of Massachusetts, I pronounce you husband and wife. Caleb, you may kiss your bride," the judge concluded.

Lauren missed her mother sobbing silently against her father's chest, the unshed tears glittering in Gwen's eyes and the triumphant gleam in Joelle Samuels's golden gaze when Cal lowered his head and covered her mouth with firm lips.

Cal gathered Lauren tightly, seemingly trying to absorb her into himself. Now he was complete, whole, and for that he had to thank Lauren.

"Thank you, darling," he whispered against her pliant mouth. "Thank you for my son and for giving him his legacy."

Lauren stiffened his embrace, her head spinning and making her faint. Cal had said nothing about loving her. *He could've lied,* she thought. At that moment even a lie would've been better than saying nothing, and she began to suspect what Cal felt for her was only passion. They were perfect in bed—their lust for each other evenly matched.

Cal covered the small hand resting on the lapel of his tuxedo jacket with his larger one, unaware of Lauren's uneasiness. He squeezed her fingers gently only relinquishing his claim when Roy held out his arms to his daughter.

Roy gathered Lauren to his chest, kissing her cheek. "You're no longer my baby, Laurie. You now belong to your husband as he belongs to you."

Lauren recovered, smiling up at her father, seeing sadness in his dark eyes. "I may be a married woman, but I'll always be your baby, Daddy."

She pulled out of her father's arms, stepping back and looping an arm through Cal's. She stood in the shadowed coolness of a large black and white striped tent ready to receive the good wishes of her family members and guests.

Odessa wanted an outdoor celebration and the weather had cooperated. The day was awash with bright sunlight, a clear sky and warm summer breezes, and Odessa's black and white silk dress emphasized the color scheme for her daughter's special day.

Lauren felt the muscles tense under Cal's arm with Andrew's approach. The attractive red-haired woman who had been Andrew's blind date clung possessively to his hand.

Andrew flashed Lauren a lopsided grin. "I knew you'd be a beautiful bride." Leaning over, he kissed her cheek. "Even though you're married, I'll still be here for you if you need me," he whispered in her ear, green eyes twinkling. He extended a hand to Cal. "My best, Caleb. I'd like you and Lauren to meet Danelle. Danelle, Caleb and Lauren Samuels."

Cal shook Andrew's hand and nodded to Danelle. "Thank you for coming."

His polite facade did not slip. He had overheard Andrew's statement to Lauren, but he didn't want to spoil his wedding day by confronting the agent about his relationship with Mrs. Caleb Samuels, and one thing Andrew Monroe would come to know was that Caleb Samuels was a selfish man, and not for any reason would he share what he considered to be his and his solely.

Lauren couldn't bring herself to eat any of the expertly prepared food. After two bites, the succulently tender filet mignon seemed to stick in her throat. She caught Cal's raised eyebrows as she reached for a glass of champagne.

Cal forced his gaze away from her revealing neckline, staring down into the velvety blackness of her large eyes. "Are you all right?"

Lauren took a swallow of the sparkling dry wine. "Yes." Her voice was low and breathless.

Cal ignored the other guests seated under the striped tent. Everyone was eating and drinking while silent waiters stood by each table.

"You're drinking and not eating," he stated flatly.

Lauren's glass was poised in midair. It was only her first glass of champagne. "Do I need your permission to drink?"

"No. But . . ."

"Then don't monitor my actions," she shot back in a quiet voice. "You have your son and your wife, Caleb. Shouldn't that be enough for you?"

Cal's features hardened. "No, it's not enough."

Her gaze raced over her husband's face. Cal was exquisite in formal dress. He had worn a black and white striped silk tie and cummerbund with his tuxedo and his graying hair appeared a gleaming silver against the loose curling black strands. Spending time outdoors with Drew had darkened his face to a healthy glowing chestnut brown.

"What do you want?" She enunciated each word.

Cal could not believe the sharpness in her tone. Her voice was low yet cutting. What had he said? What had he done to set her on edge?

Gripping her elbow tightly, he eased her up from her chair. "We need to talk."

Ignoring the inquisitive stares of their guests, Cal led Lauren out of the tent toward the house. Once inside the spacious Colonial structure he closed the front door behind them.

Pulling Lauren to his chest, Cal cupped her face in his hands. He lowered his head, tasting her mouth. "To answer your question, I want you Lauren Samuels," he murmured between nibbling kisses. "I want you and only you," he continued, then took full possession of her mouth.

Lauren pushed against the solid wall of his chest. "No, Caleb."

His hold slipped down to her tiny waist. Raising his head he stared at her. "Yes, Lauren. Drew isn't the only one I want in my life."

"You needed me to fulfill the conditions of your grandfather's will."

"I want you for you, Lauren," he refuted.

She wanted so much to believe him. She wanted to believe that he loved her and he wanted her because he loved her.

"I'll always want you, sweetheart. Even when you don't want me." He ran a finger down her throat and over her chest to the soft swell of breasts rising above the revealing décolleté.

Lauren sagged weakly against his body, closing her eyes. "What have we gotten into?" she sighed, realizing the enormity of their situation for the first time. "We've allowed someone else—a dead man—to dictate our destiny."

"My grandfather was a very wise man, darling. I have a feeling he knew exactly what he was doing when he rewrote his will."

"But we don't love each other, Cal. People who marry one another usually do it because of love and commitment," she argued softly. "Not only have we married once, but twice and it has been for all the wrong reasons."

Cal leaned back, noting the distress marring the loveliness of her delicate face. Lauren was strong, yet whenever her vulnerability surfaced it was impossible for her to conceal it from him.

A sad smile touched his mouth and he shifted a dark eyebrow. "Who knows, Lauren. Perhaps one day we'll fall in love."

"I doubt that, Caleb," she replied with a heaviness in her chest. How much more could she love him, and how was she to spend a year with him, sharing her life and offering him her body and knowing he wouldn't return her love?

"A lot can happen in a year or less." He pressed a tender kiss on her lips.

Lauren wished she could feel as confident as he did. "Perhaps you're right," she replied, inhaling. The gesture caused her breasts to rise above the beaded neckline and it was Cal's turn to inhale sharply. "I think we'd better get back to our guests or they'll think we couldn't wait to begin our honeymoon."

Cal nodded, smiling. "I don't think the honeymoon could get any better than what we've already shared," he teased.

Lauren felt her face heat up and she stared down at the

toes of her white satin pumps showing through the provocative slit.

Cal laughed openly, adding to her discomfort. Even though she had shared her bed and body with Cal, Lauren still did not feel as comfortable as she should've been whenever he teased her about their passionate lovemaking.

His arm curved possessively on her waist as he directed her out of the house and into the bright afternoon sunlight.

Lauren and Cal returned to the tent to an expressive silence, all gazes directed at them. Cal's arm tightened noticeably on her body, and he displayed a wide grin.

"Post-marital jitters," he stated, smiling down at his wife.

Lauren nodded her confirmation. "I'm okay."

The cacophony of voices started up again when Cal seated Lauren. He retook his own chair, draping a proprietary arm over the back of hers. He signaled the waiter at their table with a slight motion of his free hand.

"Mrs. Samuels needs another plate," he ordered quietly.

Within minutes a plate appeared with filet mignon, a green vegetable salad with an orange-hazelnut dressing and a zesty corn salad in a cilantro dressing.

Lauren ate most of the food, her spirits lifting. All that mattered was that she was in love with her husband, and she would spend the next year of her life with the man she loved.

After everyone had eaten their fill, the festivities moved inside. The caterers had set up long tables filled with sweet pastries and liquid refreshment. The arrival of a small combo signaled a night filled with music and dancing.

Soft light from a massive overhead chandelier in the living room shimmered off the highly waxed pale oak flooring and played off the silver in Cal's hair as he led Lauren in the first dance of the evening.

Lauren, having removed her headpiece, felt Cal's mouth on her temple as he swung her expertly into his arms. She melted against him, remembering the many dances they had shared on Cay Verde.

She felt he held her too close for propriety, but she followed his strong lead without tripping or stepping on his patent-leather dress slippers.

"Did I ever tell you that you dance very well, Mr. Samuels?" she said, smiling up at Cal the moment he relaxed his grip.

His thick dark lashes shadowed his eyes when he stared at her smiling mouth. "My mother insisted that I learn to dance. Dancing was her life and anyone in her life was swept along with it."

"I think my Uncle Odell is quite taken with your mother." Lauren peered around Cal's shoulder to find her uncle engrossed in conversation with Joelle. "His wife died two years ago," she added, noting the surprise lifting Cal's eyebrows.

"Mother has mellowed these past few years. Perhaps she won't be too hard on him."

"I've sat in my uncle's court. He can hold his own," Lauren countered with a knowing grin.

"Matchmaking, darling?" Cal queried, lowering his voice and his head.

"Of course not," she replied innocently.

"Good. Now, let's hope your agent and his red-haired girlfriend can amuse each other long enough to contemplate a legal liaison so that he can leave my wife the hell alone."

Lauren's jaw dropped, but she wasn't given the chance to reply to Cal's caustic dig at Andrew, when her father cut in to claim his dance.

* * *

The frivolity continued for hours, long after Lauren and Cal toasted each other with champagne, cut the artfully decorated three-tier wedding cake and Lauren had thrown her bouquet of cream-colored roses, tulips and orchids. Cal flashed a Cheshire-cat grin when Danelle caught the flowers and waved them in front of Andrew.

Gwen nodded to Lauren and the two women slipped away to the small guest bedroom on the second floor.

Gwen sat down on the bed, watching Lauren remove the bracelet circling her wrist. "I must say that Caleb Samuels has fab taste in jewelry." She sighed, falling back on the bed. "I'm going to enjoy writing up this wedding for my column. Especially since the bride wore an original Scaasi gown."

Lauren undid the many satin-covered buttons along the beaded sleeves. She hadn't been able to resist the stunning garment once she saw it in a Boston bridal shop.

"At first my mother thought it was a little too risqué, but I reminded her that I wasn't having a church wedding."

"I never knew Aunt Dessa was that conservative," Gwen complained. "Her own yellow dress was equally risqué with a revealing neckline and side slit." She sat up. "But could you imagine stuffy old Reverend Lewis salivating over your chest and dress. He probably would've had apoplexy before he finished the ceremony."

Lauren laughed and stepped out of the dress, changing quickly into a pair of lightweight gabardine slacks and a cotton and silk blend sweater. Gwen hugged and kissed Lauren, whispering ribald suggestions in her ear that she should consider making her honeymoon an exciting and memorable one.

Lauren's face was still burning when Cal knocked on the door and stepped into the room.

"I don't want to rush you but we do have to cover more than a hundred miles tonight."

"And you intend to make it in an hour," she teased.

"I've stopped speeding." His expression was stoic.

"Since when?" Lauren picked up a shoulder bag, making her way to the door.

He caught her arm, taking the bag. His gaze lingered on her mouth. "Since this afternoon, Lauren. It suddenly hit me that as a husband and father I have to be more responsible. I have to take care of you and Drew, therefore I can no longer afford to take the risks I used to take before."

"You don't have to take care of me," she replied.

He leaned over her. "Don't tell me what to do, Lauren." The softly spoken words were layered with steel.

Lauren felt a flicker of annoyance. They hadn't been married a day and already Cal wanted to control her, and she wondered if he was more like David Samuels than he realized.

"I am not your responsibility. Therefore, you will not have to take care of me," she stated flatly.

His mouth tightened and thinned. "Let's not argue about it."

Her large dark eyes narrowed. "Yes. Let's not."

Turning, she made her way down the hall to the staircase leading to the back of the house. Lauren didn't know why but she felt the need to argue with her husband. She wanted to release the frustrations torturing her night and day.

She wanted to tell Caleb Samuels that she loved him; she wanted to tell him that she wanted to spend not a year but the rest of her life with him, and she wanted another child.

The yearning for another baby had surfaced unexpectedly. It happened after a tender session of lovemaking when she and Cal seemed content to make the pleasure last as long as possible.

They both had tempered their passions, holding back, until fulfillment was a sweet, soaring warm release of sated ecstasy. She lay awake for hours afterwards, remembering the soft flutters in her womb whenever her unborn son moved, and she wanted to experience those sensations again.

However, Lauren knew it had to be different if she ever found herself pregnant again. This time she wanted to plan for a child, and the child had to be wanted both by her and by Cal.

They slipped out of the house unseen by anyone. Lauren thought it best they not make their departure known to Drew. She had suggested it as much for herself as for her son. The thought of leaving him for a week had gnawed at her conscience. It would be the first time she would be without him for more than two days.

Cal settled her into the sports car, closing the door with a solid slam. It was apparent that his own temper was still smarting from her statement that she was not his responsibility.

He started up the car, shifted into gear and began the westward journey across the State of Massachusetts.

"Odell has offered to escort my mother around," he stated after a lengthy silence.

Lauren's head came around and she stared at the smirk on his face. "Then I wasn't wrong. I knew he liked her."

"What else do you know?" Cal asked in the quiet tone that always sent a ripple of longing throughout her.

She frowned. "What are you talking about?"

"It appears as if you're quite perceptive about a lot of things. What else have you picked up?"

"About what?"

"Not about what, but who?"

"About who, Cal?"

"About me, Mrs. Samuels."

Lauren pulled her gaze away from the shadowy outline of his features. Night had fallen and the only light came from the glow of the dials on the dashboard and from the headlights of oncoming traffic.

She searched her memory for changes in Cal since the day they had met again at the attorney's office, but came up blank. He was usually even-tempered and relaxed, and she knew he didn't like Andrew.

"I don't know, Cal," she admitted. "You tell me."

Cal let out his breath slowly, shaking his head. "No, Lauren. I won't tell you. If you don't know by now, then you'll never know."

His fingers gripped the steering wheel savagely. Didn't she know? How could she not know that he loved her? When he made love to her he not only gave her his body but also his spirit. He gave her everything he had, leaving himself naked and vulnerable to the pain that Lauren and only Lauren could inflict.

Both of them wrestled with their private demons as the sleek Porsche ate up the highway, Cal concentrating on his driving while Lauren closed her eyes.

"Wake up, darling. We're here."

Lauren woke immediately. "I'm sorry I wasn't much company,' she apologized with a delicate yawn.

Cal smiled, noting her heavy lids. "You needed the rest. You've been through a lot."

Lauren placed her hand in Cal's and he pulled her gently from the car. She leaned against his chest and he cradled her body to his, offering his warmth. The air in the mountains was cool at night.

"We've both been through a lot, Cal," she mumbled, snuggling in the crisp cotton of his pale blue denim shirt.

"And now it's time we think about offering each other a measure of happiness, *querida.*" He rested his chin on the top of her head. "My grandfather may have forced us back into each other's lives but that doesn't mean we can't make this marriage of convenience work."

Pulling back, Lauren stared up at him. She registered his plea, but the darkness would not permit her to see his features clearly. She wanted so much to see the tenderness emanating from the smoldering depths of his fire-lit eyes.

Lauren opened her mouth to blurt out her love for him, then at the last moment bit down on her lower lip to swallow back her confession. She would not tell him; not yet.

Rising on tiptoe, she kissed his mouth. Her lips told him what her tongue wouldn't as she kissed him with all the emotion she could summon for her husband.

Cal's heart thudded wildly against her breasts, and Lauren knew by the obvious changes in his body that he desired her.

"Let's go inside," he gasped, breathing heavily in her ear.

Chapter Twelve

This wedding night was different from the one they had shared on Cay Verde. Lauren came to Cal with a passion that was strong, uncomplicated and boundless in its intensity.

Five years ago she had been innocent and ignorant—innocent in that she wasn't very experienced or worldly, and ignorant of her very passionate nature.

No man had ever been able to reach inside of her to erase the inhibition she wore like a shield of honor. No man but Caleb Samuels.

Lauren had stopped asking herself why she couldn't resist Cal. Each time they came together she felt as if she renewed her life cycle.

Hands, mouths, tongues caressed and tasted nakedness until Cal and Lauren grew impatient to sample the oneness that transported them to a private sphere where they ceased to exist as separate entities.

Lauren's decision to use an oral contraceptive provided both of them with a maximum pleasure they hadn't thought possible.

Gritting his teeth, Cal called on all of his control not to give into the rush of ecstasy spiraling wildly with each thrust into his wife's tight, hot body.

Lauren wrapped her legs around his waist and gave herself up to the hysteria of delight ravaging her mind and body. If she couldn't tell Cal that she loved him, then her body would. Each and every time she lay with him she whispered silently over and over that she loved him.

She surrendered completely to the sensations straining for release and she gasped in the shattering, explosive pleasure, clinging to Cal when she felt him also surrender to the forces dissolving their captive hearts.

Smiling, Lauren gloried in the light kisses raining on her face and mouth, then feathering over the rapidly beating pulse along the column of her neck.

An aching tingling lingered in her breasts and between her thighs. Moving slightly she felt Cal stir within her body and she moaned sensually.

"Are you all right?" he asked breathlessly.

Lauren moaned again. "I'm fine, darling."

She was better than fine. A soothing, comforting feeling of banked fires, passion and love swept over her as she drifted off to sleep.

Lauren descended the staircase, following the distinctive aroma of brewing coffee. She had discovered upon waking that the house in the mountains was anything but rustic. Constructed of glass, wood and stone, it sat on a rise overlooking a small lake. It was the perfect retreat for a writer or artist who craved solitude.

Her bare feet did not warn Cal of her approach as she made her way into a spacious sun-filled kitchen.

Cal sat at a bleached pine table, feet anchored on a chair while his fingers raced quickly over a laptop computer. She moved into his line of vision and he glanced up, a tender smile softening his mouth and smoothing out the lines of concentration in his forehead.

"Good morning, Mrs. Samuels. I can say that now, without you going for my throat," he teased.

Lauren floated to his side, winding her arms around his

neck. "Good morning, Mr. Samuels." Her mint-flavored breath whispered over his awaiting lips.

Cal placed the laptop on the table, pulling Lauren down to his lap. "Are you ready for breakfast?"

She glanced up at the clock over the sink. It was past noon. She had slept away all of the morning. "I think brunch would be more like it."

The fingers of Cal's right hand were splayed over her flat belly while his left played in the thick glossy curls around her ears that Lauren had managed to control with the assistance of a curling iron.

He remembered the tousled curls scattered over her head in sensual disarray when he awoke earlier that morning. He lay beside her, watching her as she slept and wondering what dark secrets she kept from him. He found it hard to believe that Lauren could come to him so willingly, offering her body in total abandon while withholding any hint of deeper feelings for him; he pondered whether their relationship was destined always to be one-dimensional. Would they share only Drew and their passions?

"I'd much prefer dessert," he replied with a teasing grin.

Lauren laughed lightly. "Brunch first, Caleb Samuels."

He stuck out his lower lip, pouting. "But I want dessert." Lauren pulled out of his embrace, standing up with hands on her hips. She gave him the *look*. He rose with her. "All right, warden, brunch first."

They ate brunch at a restaurant that catered to family-style dining. Most of the patrons were dressed in jeans, sweats or jogging attire.

After dining, Cal gave Lauren a tour of the square block of the business area that featured a mini-market, gift shop, bank, post office and service station. They bought

staples to stock the refrigerator and pantry and returned
to the house for an afternoon of boating.

"Don't rock the boat, Lauren," Cal warned as he
dipped the canoe paddle in the clear lake water.

Lauren anchored her hands on the sides of the canoe
and swayed. "What's the matter, Caleb?" she taunted.
"Can't you swim?"

Cal pulled the paddle into the boat. "Of course I can
swim. Can you, darling?"

She was never given the opportunity to reply. Cal
tipped the canoe, spilling both of them into the cold
water. Lauren sputtered and splashed water while trying
to hold onto the overturned boat.

"Caleb!"

Cal was beside her in seconds, holding her up. "I won't
let you drown."

Lauren pushed against his chest. "I won't drown. I can
swim," she rasped, treading water.

Cal righted the canoe, flipping agilely into it. He extended a hand and pulled Lauren after him.

"You ruined my hair," she wailed, patting the water-
soaked strands.

He gave her a baleful glance. "You look beautiful."

Lauren sniffed loudly. "If I looked like a toad you'd say
that I look beautiful," she grumbled.

Cal's expression changed. "Damn right." His grin
slipped away when he noticed the outline of her bare
breasts under her wet T-shirt. He hadn't lied to her. She
was beautiful. With or without her clothes—wet or dry,
and he suspected she didn't know just how beautiful and
sexy she was without even trying.

He loved the rich dark brown of her skin, the thick
blackness of her hair and the velvety serenity of her dark
eyes. He admired her feminine fragility and her grace. He
welcomed her calming spirit and respected her intellect.

"Thank you, Gramps," he mumbled under his breath. "Did you say something?"

Cal shook his head and continued paddling, unaware that Lauren's fingers trailed in the water, skimming over large floating lilies. Without warning, she scooped up a handful of water, splashing his face.

"You're going to pay for that stunt," he threatened softly, blinking through droplets. Cal jumped out of the canoe as soon as it touched shallow water, pulling it up on the soggy bank.

He reached for Lauren, but she had slipped from the boat with the quickness of a wood nymph, running toward the house.

Cal's longer legs caught up with her and he wrestled her to the grassy lawn. The heat from his body burned through their wet clothes.

His weight held her captive as he lowered his head to claim her mouth in a kiss that was more of a reward than punishment.

"I want you, baby," he confessed, pressing his lips to her closed eyelids. "I want you so much it frightens me." His tongue traced the length of her nose before he took her mouth again.

Lauren, relishing the sweetness of his mouth, arched, making him aware that she was ready to accept him.

The waning rays of the late afternoon sun warmed her limbs as he removed her wet clothing, exposing her to the quiet, private beauty of the countryside.

Cal did not protest as Lauren helped him out of his wet shirt and shorts, then straddled him.

There on the grass, in full view of nature's majesty, they made love. It was slow, unhurried and profoundly satisfying.

They waited until their breathing resumed its normal rate before returning to the house, both of them changed by the uninhibited act.

Lauren did not want Cal to leave her, and she waited for the right time to tell him.

The time never seemed right and Lauren decided to enjoy her husband and all that he offered her. The seclusion of the large house afforded them the privacy she sought, and when the weather proved hot enough she and Cal swam with a minimum of clothing, then made love under the sun or the stars.

She and Cal prepared sumptuous dishes under the summer skies, broiling steaks, lobster tails or freshly caught trout on an outdoor grill. The days and nights blurred and with the passing of time Lauren fell more and more in love with Cal.

A tiny voice whispered incessantly that Cal loved her, but somehow Lauren couldn't bring herself to believe it.

Lauren pulled a lightweight blanket up to Drew's chin. "Go to sleep, darling," she urged in a low, soothing tone. "You'll be able to ride your bike again in the morning."

"Okay," Drew said around a yawn.

She kissed his forehead. "God bless. I love you."

Drew's eyes closed. "Love you, too," he slurred before sleep claimed his exhausted body.

Lauren sighed in relief. She and Cal had only been back two days, but it had taken every minute to undo the haphazard schedule Odessa had afforded her grandson.

She wanted to reprimand her mother for permitting Drew to stay up hours beyond his scheduled nap and bedtime. Then there were the forbidden foods: potato chips, jelly apples, bubble gum, French fries and soda. Odessa had given her a sheepish grin, saying it had been a special week.

Lauren adjusted Drew's night-light and made her way

down the staircase where Cal sat talking with his mother on the front porch.

Pushing open the screen door, she stepped out into the magical darkness of the hot summer night. Cal rose and seated her on the swing. The golden light from porch lamps was flattering to her delicate features.

"How about something cold to drink, darling?" he asked, leaning over and inhaling her floral scent.

Lauren ran a hand over her moist cheek. "Yes, please," she replied with a warm smile.

Cal straightened. "What would you like, Mother?"

"Just water thank you, Caleb."

Joelle had closely observed her son with his new bride since their return. She recognized something about him that had never been apparent before: a calming spirit. Gone was the self-imposed control that never seemed to slip, and the cold remoteness in his sun-lit eyes had also disappeared.

"Don't hurt him, Lauren," Joelle said quietly after Cal disappeared into the house.

Lauren stared at Joelle. The older woman was sprawled gracefully on the chaise. "Why would I do that, Joelle?"

"I don't think you would deliberately hurt my son, but it could happen because he loves you," Joelle explained. "He may not have loved you the first time you married but it's different now. And knowing that he's a father has also changed him."

Lauren couldn't help notice the tingle of excitement within her at her mother-in-law's statement; but she knew better than anyone that Cal did not love her.

"I won't hurt my husband," she declared adamantly, adding silently, how could they not help but hurt each other when their year ended. Neither of them would escape unscathed.

"Thank you, Lauren." Joelle appeared deep in thought before she spoke again. "I caused David more pain than he deserved. He loved me, Lauren," she confessed. "He loved me so much that he never had anything left for his son. And that's all Caleb ever wanted from him—his love."

"Why did you move to Spain?" Lauren questioned.

"Vanity," Joelle answered as honestly as she could. "The principal dancer in my dance troupe became ill one night and as her understudy I filled in for her as Carmen. The next morning I was touted as the Josephine Baker of Barcelona. It all went to my head and when the troupe left Spain for France, I stayed.

"I was twenty when I met David Samuels for the first time. I'd returned to the States for a tour and he had come to see me dance. He followed me from state to state, begging me to marry him. I laughed and told him I was too young but he wouldn't give up. I returned to Europe four months later, hoping I could forget him but it wasn't that easy. My concentration was off and my performances suffered. The director of the company sent me back home to recuperate, but instead of going to Baton Rouge I went to Boston.

"I barged into a meeting that David was chairing and crooked my finger at him. I thought he was going to faint when he saw me and he politely excused himself. I told him I was prepared to dance for him—every night if he would marry me."

"Why did you wait so long to marry him?"

Joelle managed a small smile. "I see you know the story." Lauren nodded. "I felt I had to have total and complete control of my life, but that wasn't easy with David. He was unyielding—all or nothing. He was dogmatic that we name our son after his father. I only gave in because I was too depressed after having the baby to fight him."

"Knowing this you married him twice," Lauren said in awe.

"I had to get him out of my system. And when I left him the second time I knew it was finally over."

Cal returned with a tray of lemonade and sparkling water and the conversation came to an abrupt end.

Lauren, Cal and Joelle sat on the porch laughing and talking until the older woman pleaded fatigue. She said she had to be up early because she and Odell had planned to visit Cape Cod before she returned to Spain.

Neither Cal nor Lauren mentioned a possible liaison between Joelle and the widowed judge. Both of them were too concerned with their own futures.

Chapter Thirteen

Lauren focused her attention on Drew. The child was shoveling food into his mouth as quickly as he could chew and swallow each forkful.

"Don't eat so fast, Drew," she warned.

Drew mumbled something unintelligible, his mouth filled with rice and snow peas.

"Swallow your food, then talk," Cal suggested.

Drew chewed, his gaze darting from his mother's to his father's smiling face. "I have to eat fast and go to bed." The words rushed out after he had swallowed the remains of his dinner. "Daddy says I have to get up early to go fishing or the fish don't bite when it's late. I told Missy to have Bandit go to bed early so he won't be tired when we're ready to leave."

"If Bandit's sleepy I'm certain he'll sleep in the van," Lauren replied, hoping to reassure her son that the frisky puppy would survive his first outing away from the house.

Drew wiped his mouth with a napkin, then assumed the posture of resting his elbows on the table and cradling his chin on the heels of his hands. He waited for his parents to dismiss him from the table.

Lauren thought the gesture was one Drew was comfortable with until she realized Cal also rested his chin on his hands whenever he was deep in thought. It always amazed her how much the two of them were alike—in looks and gestures.

Cal made an expressive flourish of wiping his mouth with his napkin, placing it alongside his plate. He glanced down at his watch.

"I think it's time we home boys turn in so we can get up early for our trip." He punctuated his words with a yawn. "Can you take care of the dishes, darling?" Only Lauren saw him wink.

Drew mimicked his father, stretching and yawning. "Little homey sure is tired."

Lauren smothered a smile when Drew referred to himself as "little homey." Father and son had become the Grafton Home Boys and Cal differentiated between the home boys by calling Drew little homey.

She waved a delicate hand at her husband and son. "I think I'll be able to manage."

Drew scrambled from his chair, circling the table to pull back Lauren's chair. He had seen Cal do it, and lately he'd imitated his father's every gesture.

"Daddy and I will help you with the dishes when we come back. Promise," he added, his large eyes brimming with excitement.

Lauren leaned down and kissed Drew's cheek. "Thank you, sweetheart."

Drew's arms curved and tightened around her neck. He placed a noisy kiss on her cheek. "Good night, Mommy."

"I'll see you later," Cal whispered to Lauren.

She blew him a kiss before clearing the table. A small smile played around her mouth. Cal and Drew were about to embark on their first fishing trip while she had made her own plans to spend the weekend in Boston. Cal had agreed to take Missy and Bandit, thereby permitting her complete freedom.

Humming to herself, Lauren quickly cleaned the kitchen. She and Cal had been married for two months and it appeared as if their hunger for each other would never abate.

They made love at night, early in the morning, and there were times when they both took time away from their work to seek the other out during the day whenever Drew was at school. Lauren continued to do her research in her attic retreat while Cal elected to use the sun porch at the rear of the house for his writing.

Cal did not talk to her about his writing except to solicit her input on a historical fact. The times he joined her in bed, hours after she had retired, he came with repressed tensions that carried over to his lovemaking; only after he'd spilled out his passion did reason and sanity reign for the two of them.

The kitchen cleaned, Lauren made her way upstairs. She heard Cal's and Drew's voices in the child's bedroom, and she smiled. Cal was readying Drew for bed.

Their sharing the responsibility of looking after Drew allowed Lauren more free time for herself than she had had in the past, and she knew even after their year together ended Cal was certain to continue his involvement with his son.

Lauren entered her bedroom and headed to the adjoining bath. This was one night when she'd be able to enjoy a leisurely bath.

Filling the tub with warm water, she added scented bath crystals, then brushed her teeth and cleansed her face before slipping off her clothes and stepping into the bathtub. Sliding down into the silken bubbles, she sighed.

Lauren closed her eyes and lay in the bathtub until the water cooled and the bubbles disappeared. She opened her eyes and discovered Cal leaning against the door, arms crossed over his chest.

She sank down deeper in the water, heat stealing into her cheeks. "How long have you been standing there?"

His smile was sardonic. "Long enough to see *enough.*" He reached for a thick, thirsty bath sheet, and held it out to her. "I put Drew to bed and now it's time for his mother."

Moving closer, Cal waited for Lauren to stand, and draped the bath sheet around her water-slicked body. He lifted her from the tub and carried her into the bedroom.

"You're wetting the bed," Lauren protested as he laid her on the crisp sheets.

Cal stripped away the towel and covered her body with his. "It doesn't matter, baby. One way or the other it still will get wet," he breathed into her mouth.

Lauren moaned softly when his hands began a gentle exploration of her naked body. She began her own exploration, helping to relieve him of his clothing.

"You started this," she hissed between clenched teeth, "and I intend to finish it."

Cal pulled her over his body, smiling up at her. "You won't get a fight from me."

Straddling his thighs, Lauren settled herself over his rigid flesh. The swift, smooth motion elicited a moan from the both of them.

"Cal . . . oh, Caleb," she gasped, her desire spiraling out of control. The fires were now fever-pitched and Lauren knew there would be no prolonged bout of love-making this night.

Cal watched the play of differing emotions on his wife's face. There was never a need for her to fake her responses. He felt every fiber of her as if they shared the same body.

He cupped her breasts, thumbs sweeping over her distended nipples. Closing his eyes, Cal let his senses take over. He felt her soft, wet flesh sheathing his, heard her quickly rising labored breathing, inhaled her distinctive feminine fragrance and tasted her silky flesh.

"Lauren," he groaned aloud when she pressed her breasts to his chest, her hips moving rhythmically against his. "Please, baby. Don't torture me!" he gasped.

Lauren buried her face between his neck and shoulder, quickening her rhythm. "Let it go, Caleb. Please!"

Cal's arms tightened around her body. "No!" He wanted it to last—forever if that was possible.

"Please, darling," she pleaded.

He thought their lovemaking couldn't get any better but it had. Each time Lauren offered herself to him he treasured the joining as a gift and a reward; a reward for his loving her.

But he had to let it go. Either that or he would go crazy.

His release was strong, hot and wildly exciting, as was Lauren's, and he bit down on his lower lip to keep from embarrassing himself.

He loved her; he loved Lauren enough to give up his life for her, and at that moment he did because for a few seconds he experienced what the French call *le petit mort*.

Cal's hands cradled the soft fullness of her bottom as he placed light kisses on her moist temple. *"Te amo, querida,"* he whispered against her ear. "I love you, darling," he translated into English.

Lauren lay motionless, only the beating of her heart indicating she was still alive. Total satisfaction and fulfillment vibrated throughout her entire being.

His declaration of love was lost to her for she had retreated into a cocoon of a sated, dreamless sleep.

Cal eased Lauren's form down beside him and covered her with the sheet. His gaze caressed her lovingly as he examined the woman who had been fated to him.

Reaching up, he flicked off the lamp and turned to Lauren, pulling her gently to his side.

"I love you, Lauren Samuels."

Knowing he could say it aloud lifted his spirits to soaring heights, and he couldn't wait to tell her.

Cal slipped quietly from the bed, hours before threads of light lined the dark sky. He listened to Lauren's soft even breathing, deciding not to wake her and curbing his desire to kiss her. He would kiss her and tell her how much he loved her when he and Drew returned from their weekend fishing outing.

He used the guest bedroom to wash and dress, then woke Drew, whispering softly to the child not to make any noise that would wake his mother.

It was four-thirty by the time Cal urged Missy into a minivan. He picked up the whining, wiggling puppy and placed it in the large space behind the fold-down rear seats.

Drew adjusted his shoulder harness and seat belt, unable to quell his excitement as he was to embark on what he considered to be the best event of his young life thus far. He'd predicted that it was going to be better than celebrating his fourth birthday.

Cal slipped into the van, turned on the engine, then secured his seat belt. Glancing quickly at Drew, he smiled. He was about to share with his son what David Samuels had never shared with him, and he was grateful that he had been given a second chance at life—a chance to have a meaningful relationship with his son and a chance to discover love and happiness with a woman he wanted to share the rest of his life with.

"Ready, little homey?"

"Yeah!" Drew replied in a loud whisper.

"Well, let's go."

Cal backed out of the garage, with Drew acting as navigator so they wouldn't bump or scrape Lauren's car. He winked at Drew, giving him a thumbs-up sign before they gave each other high-fives.

*   *   *

Lauren rolled over to the opposite side of her bed and woke up. His body was missing, his heat had evaporated, however his scent remained. Reaching over, she hugged the cold pillow. Cal had left without waking her.

Stretching languidly, Lauren arched her feet, extending her arms above her head. The weekend was hers and hers alone. She had planned a shopping outing along Boston's Newbury Street, then she was to meet Gwen and their friends at a popular upscale supper club for an informal gathering.

She noted the time on the bedside clock and practically jumped from the bed. She had wanted to be on the road by ten to avoid the crush of Saturday morning traffic.

Lauren complimented herself when she showered, dressed and backed her car out of the driveway within forty-five minutes. Cal's Porsche was parked in a corner of the garage. The two-seat vehicle was a constant reminder of his former bachelor days for he now referred to himself as a family man, and within two months they had become a stable nuclear family: father, mother and child.

Concentrating on her driving, Lauren refused to think of when it would all end. She had promised herself that she would not think about what was to happen the following August because she was too in love with Cal to permit a thread of apprehension or disappointment shatter her world of enchanted contentment.

Lauren wound her way through the throng standing shoulder-to-shoulder at the bar in Off the Beaten Path. The club's name was totally incongruent to its location. It was in the heart of downtown Boston and had become a favorite hangout for anyone in publishing.

An attractive man with a modified fade and luminous dark eyes blocked Lauren's path. His gaze swept appreciably over her face and body.

"Looking for me?" he asked, displaying a sexy smile.

She couldn't help but return his smile. "I don't think so." She tried stepping around him, but he wouldn't move.

"You here alone?"

Lauren sighed heavily, running a hand through her hair. He caught the flash of bright lights from her rings, nodding. "So the pretty young honey is taken," he crooned. "You should tell your old man not to let you walk around looking this sweet unless he's attached to some part of your fine little body." He made a big show of stepping aside to let her pass.

Lauren spied Gwen and waved to her. Her cousin was sitting at a table with two other women.

Gwen stood up, hands braced on her hips. "I see you still have it, girl."

Lauren hugged and kissed her cousin. "I hope you're not talking about Don Juan." She crooked her thumb in the direction of her spurned admirer.

"The brother truly has the gift for gab. I think of him as a walking greeting card," Gwen whispered in her ear.

"I think I'll stick with Caleb Samuels," Lauren admitted with a wide grin.

"Who wouldn't prefer C. B. Samuels," a youthful-looking reporter from the *Boston Gazette* crooned, hugging Lauren when she sat down.

Lauren greeted the book editor from Summit with a wave and a warm smile. "How's life at the top?"

The woman's face brightened. "I'm breathing rarefied

air. I'm still not used to being associate editor of the textbook division."

The conversation turned to publishing news and Lauren felt as if she had never left Summit when she was brought up-to-date on the events at the book company. It had been a long time—too long since she had been out with the "girls."

Over drinks and an assortment of entrées and appetizers the conversation shifted to boyfriends, husbands and failed relationships.

The noise level escalated as loudspeakers blared the latest hits, and Lauren found she had to shout to be heard even by those seated nearest her.

"Now, there's one sex muffin I'd like to take a bite out of," Gwen mumbled to Lauren.

Following the direction of Gwen's gaze, Lauren went still. She recognized Jacqueline Samuels with the object of Gwen's admiration, missing the breadth of the man's wide shoulders, deep copper-brown complexion, perfect white teeth as he smiled, a mobile male mouth, strong chin and the tilting slant of coal black eyes when her eyes locked with those of the woman clinging possessively to his arm.

"Something wrong, cuz?" Gwen asked, registering the stillness in Lauren.

"That's Jackie Samuels," she replied quietly.

"He looks a little young for her," Gwen mused aloud as Jacqueline directed her escort toward their table.

"I don't think many things bother the lady if she's out to get a man," Lauren remarked.

Jacqueline stopped at their table, tightening her hold on the massive upper arm covered in creamy cashmere. Her gaze darted quickly over Lauren's expertly coiffed hair, tasteful makeup that complemented a shocking pink silk shirt she had paired with a short slim forest-green suede skirt and matching green suede shoes.

"Isn't it nice that Caleb let his little wife out for the night," Jacqueline sneered. She glanced around. "Or is he here babysitting you?"

Lauren stood, facing the woman and curbing her impulse to slap her blind, swallowing back the words threatening to spill from her tongue. She did not want to stoop to Jacqueline's level by trading vicious barbs.

Lauren's anger faded quickly when she saw a male figure move behind Jacqueline. "I'm here with *him*." She motioned with her chin.

On cue, Andrew Monroe strolled over to Lauren, resting both hands on her shoulders. Jacqueline licked her vermilion-colored lips, wrinkling her nose, and concluded with, "What a naughty, naughty little girl you are." She patted her escort's thick shoulder. "Let's go, lovey. We must circulate."

Letting out her breath, Lauren turned to Andrew. She found his brilliant dark green eyes crinkling in amusement.

"Thanks."

Andrew dropped an arm over her shoulders, kissing her cheek. "You're quite welcome."

Everyone at the table stared at Lauren and Andrew. "Aren't you going to introduce us to your friend, Lauren?" the Summit book editor asked, giving Andrew an admiring look.

Lauren held Andrew's hand, smiling. "Nikki, Kai, and, of course, Gwen. Ladies, my agent Andrew Monroe."

"Hello, Andrew," the three women chorused as one. Andrew laughed and blushed attractively under his tan.

"What are you doing here on a Saturday night without a date?" Lauren questioned after Andrew pulled up a chair and seated himself next to her.

"I'm waiting for Danelle. She had to fill in for a nurse who called in sick. I told her I'd meet her here," he explained, visually admiring Lauren's smiling face. "Marriage agrees with you, my friend," he added in a quiet tone.

Raising her chin, Lauren sighed, smiling. "Thank you. I recommend you try it."

"Slow down, Lauren. I haven't known Dani that long."

She affected a moue, peering at him from under her lashes. "Who mentioned Danelle?"

Andrew blushed again, lowering his head, then without warning he stood up. "You owe me a dance, Mrs. Samuels," he said quickly, hoping to make up for his faux pas. "I never got the chance to dance with you at your wedding."

Lauren wasn't given the chance to protest as Andrew pulled her from the chair and steered her to the dance floor. The throbbing sound of a slow dance number flowed through speakers hidden in the walls as couples swayed intimately to the hypnotic composition.

Lauren enjoyed dancing with Andrew, but at that moment she wished Cal were there instead. She was as familiar with every line of her husband's body as she was with her own.

Closing her eyes, she pretended she was back on Cay Verde in Cal's arms and loving him unselfishly, and unknowingly her look of love was captured by those who were not able to see what lay buried deep within her heart.

The number ended and Andrew escorted Lauren back to the table, then took turns dancing with each woman in their party, charming them until Danelle's bright hair caught his attention. He introduced Danelle and hurriedly escorted her out of the club for their own private party.

Lauren left Off the Beaten Path after midnight and drove back to the town house. She was grateful for the Boston residence, having grown very attached to the spacious rooms and furnishings.

A slender figure jumped at her from the shadows as she placed her key in the front-door lock. "I was hoping you'd show up here."

Lauren gasped, recognizing the hard, raspy feminine voice. Anger replaced her shock as she stared at Jacqueline Samuels. "What do you want?"

Jacqueline moved under the stream of the outdoor light. Seeing her this close, under the unflattering light, Lauren did not find Jacqueline as beautiful as she originally thought. There was a hardness around her eyes and mouth that may have indicated too many late nights and perhaps too many men.

"I need to talk to you, Lauren."

"I think not," Lauren replied.

"I think I do," Jacqueline shot back, her voice hardening even more. When she knew she had Lauren's attention, she continued, "I think you ought to know something about your husband that could possibly save you from future heartache."

Lauren removed the key from the lock, slipping it into her jacket pocket. "Why should you concern yourself with my well-being?"

Jacqueline licked her lips, reminding Lauren of a cat who had just eaten her fill. "We sisters must stick together."

"You're not my sister."

"Well, not in the literal sense. I just want you to be careful with Caleb Samuels."

Lauren was tempted to unlock the door and leave Jacqueline where she stood. But on the other hand she wanted—no, needed—to hear what Jacqueline wanted to warn her about.

"Say what you have to say, then get out of here."

"Caleb slept with me when I was married to his father."

Lauren brushed past Jacqueline. "Good night."

"Ask him, little girl," Jacqueline called out to her back. "Ask him whose baby I was carrying when I married his father. Ask him if I had carried to term whether the baby would've been his son or his brother. Ask him, little girl!" she screamed.

Lauren managed to fit the key in the lock and turn it with trembling fingers. She opened and closed the door, groping through a fog of anguish, as pain lodged in her chest, threatening to make her sick.

"Liar," she whispered, closing her eyes. "She's lying." She had to be lying, Lauren thought.

But what if Jacqueline wasn't lying?

Lauren held her head with both hands, pressing the heels against her temples. She didn't want to think— couldn't think. Not now.

But she would take Jacqueline's suggestion and ask Cal. All she had to do was wait.

"Mommy, look what we got for you!"

Lauren held out her arms to her son, accepting his noisy, moist kiss on her cheek. She ran a hand over his curling hair. "Fish?"

Drew's cheeks were flushed with high color. "No . . . I mean yes. We got fish and something else." He disappeared into the house, the screen door slapping loudly against the frame.

Lauren crossed her arms over her chest, watching Cal unload the minivan. Don't let it be true, she pleaded to herself.

Missy jumped from the van, barking for her puppy to follow her lead. The rounded ball of black and white fur rolled out of the van, landing on Cal's feet.

Cal reached into the van and carefully withdrew a small bundle. He made his way toward Lauren, one hand hidden behind his back.

She moved off the porch in a short, jerky motion, resembling a marionette being pulled by different strings. A little cry escaped her parted lips when Cal thrust a kitten at her.

"No! Caleb, you didn't."

He pulled back, cradling the kitten to his chest. "Drew wanted it."

Lauren felt like crying. "Drew?"

"Well, the both of us," he admitted.

"Caleb." She struggled not to lose her temper. "My home is beginning to resemble a zoo. I get rid of one puppy and you bring home a kitten. We have one very big dog and one puppy who'll soon grow up and also be a very big dog. I don't need another animal."

Cal's free hand went to her waist, pulling her to him. "I'm away from you for two days and I don't get a kiss or an I miss you." He pressed his unshaven cheek to her silken jaw, searching for her mouth.

"Stop it!" She pushed against his chest. "You're hurting me. Besides, you smell like fish."

Cal released her, his eyes wide in surprise. "I suppose I would smell like fish if I've been fishing."

She studied his face unhurriedly, wanting to see what it was that made her fall in love with him, and she wanted to see if she could identify the evil that would permit him to sleep with his father's wife.

Without saying another word, Lauren turned on her heel and headed back to the house.

"Can Drew keep the cat?" Cal called out to her back.

Lauren stopped, fists clenched tightly. "I don't care, Caleb. I don't care about anything you do." She walked into the house, closing the door behind her.

Cal stared at the door, lines of concern creasing his forehead. Something was wrong with Lauren. He had noticed the strain in her voice and the stiffness in her body. What had happened to her in his absence?

He decided to shave and shower before seeking her out. If something was wrong he had to right it. He loved her and it was time he told her.

Chapter Fourteen

Cal slipped into the bed next to Lauren, smiling. Her eyes were closed, her breathing deep and even, but he knew she wasn't asleep.

He had waited as long as he could before coming to bed, hoping to give her a chance to work through whatever was bothering her.

Tonight she wore an ethereal white cotton nightgown with full flowing sleeves and a scooped neckline edged with delicate white lace. She had brushed her hair until it was smooth and shiny, while her face glistened with a fresh, clean innocence.

Leaning over, Cal turned off the lamp. "Are you still angry about the kitten?"

There was silence.

"Are you angry because Drew and I went off without you?"

More silence.

Cal sat up and flicked on the lamp. "Damn it, Lauren! What the hell is going on?"

Lauren rolled over and sat up. Her black eyes were burning like polished onyx. "It's you, Caleb," she rasped. "I need to know if you slept with Jacqueline while she was married to your father."

"What!" The single word exploded from Cal's mouth as his luminous eyes widened in astonishment.

"Answer my question, Caleb," she demanded.

"I will not," Cal countered.

"Then it's true." Lauren fought back tears.

"Hell no, it's not true."

Lauren pounded the bed with both fists. "Then tell me, Cal. Tell me you didn't sleep with her." Her eyes, filling with tears, overflowed.

Pulling her to his chest, Cal kissed her cheeks. "I never slept with Jacqueline, darling." His hands made soothing motions on her back. "I wouldn't sleep with that woman if she was the only one left on the planet."

"She said she slept with you and you got her pregnant," Lauren half-cried and half-laughed against his bare chest.

"Jacqueline would never permit herself to get pregnant, Lauren. She hates children."

"How do you know that?" Lauren eased back and stared up at her husband.

"She's the oldest of seven children and she always had to look out for her younger brothers and sisters. She listed children as her pet peeve in her high-school yearbook."

"How do you know this?"

He sighed heavily before continuing. "She told me this one night when she was drunk. In fact she told me her life story. The sad thing is that she woke up the next morning unaware that she had disclosed some very intimate details about her childhood."

"You dated Jacqueline?"

"Of course not, Lauren. I met her at a party and she sort of latched onto me for the night. She was a singer trying to make it in the recording field. I told her that I'd introduce her to my father who could possibly put her in touch with a few producers and that was that. The next thing I heard was that my father had married her."

"She told me you had slept with her."

"When?"

"Last night."

Cal grasped Lauren's upper arms, holding her tightly. "She came here?"

"No. She was waiting for me at the house in Boston."

"What else did she say?"

"Nothing else. Just that you had slept with her."

Cal mumbled a savage curse under his breath, then crushed Lauren to his body, not permitting her to draw a normal breath.

"Cal, you're hurting me," Lauren gasped.

He loosened his grip. "I'm sorry, darling. It's just that I don't trust Jacqueline, and I love you too much to have anything happen to you."

"You what?" She could hardly lift her voice above a whisper. Had he said what she thought he said.

"I love you, Lauren Samuels."

This time the tears that filled her eyes were tears of joy. "Say it again, Caleb Samuels."

Cal eased her down to the pillow, his smiling face looming above hers. "I love you, Lauren Taylor-Samuels."

She returned his smile. "And I love you, my husband."

Reaching over, Cal turned off the lamp and he demonstrated wordlessly how much he truly did love her.

"Caleb," Lauren cried out as she rushed into the enclosed sun porch. "Bandit chased Scrap up a tree."

Cal pushed a key, storing what he had put into his laptop and followed Lauren.

The kitten and puppy who usually got along well had begun to wreck havoc. The large puppy couldn't resist teasing the kitten whenever it wanted to sleep, resulting in the cat inflicting numerous scratches on the dog's sensitive nose.

"I'm going to get rid of both of them," Cal mumbled angrily under his breath when he saw the frightened kitten on an upper branch of the tree. "Either they learn to get along or they're going to . . ."

"To what, Caleb?" Lauren crooned, pushing the sleeves to her sweater up to her elbows. "They're beasts, animals, not children," she snapped. "You can't reason with them like you do with Drew."

"Damn the beasts," he grumbled, measuring up the tree.

"Get a ladder, Cal," she warned when she realized what he intended to do.

"The ladder will only reach so far, Lauren."

Bending slightly, he jumped up and caught hold of a lower branch and pulled himself up, his legs curving around the limb.

"Don't move, Scrap. Daddy's coming." The kitten responded, moving further away from Cal, his back arched in fear. "Stay put!" Cal shouted.

"Don't yell at him," Lauren admonished ten feet below Cal.

"Here kitty, kitty." His teeth were clenched as he inched higher and higher, praying the branches would support his weight.

Cal cursed to himself. Lauren was right, but he loath to admit it. The puppy and kitten had become twin packages of trouble. Unlike Missy, Bandit did not want to stay outdoors. He whined until he was allowed into the house, and once in he chased and teased Scrap relentlessly. Most times Lauren enjoyed their antics, but then there were times when even Drew complained that they made too much noise.

"Be careful, Cal," Lauren called out softly, lines of worry creasing her forehead.

"Stay, Scrap. Stay, Scrap," Cal repeated over and over. It seemed like hours instead of minutes as he made his way gingerly up the tree. One branch dipped dangerously and the kitten fell, landing agilely on its feet. But Cal was not as fortunate as the feline. He fell to the ground, landing with a solid thump as Scrap scampered toward the house.

Lauren was beside Cal in seconds, swallowing back her fear. Her fingers raced frantically over his face.

"Caleb?" She hardly recognized her own weak, trembling voice.

Cal's eyelids fluttered and he managed a small smile. "Hello, precious." Lauren's fingers grazed the swelling lump over his left eye and he sucked in his breath. "Don't touch it," he warned, closing his eyes.

Lauren jerked her fingers away. "Don't move, Caleb," she ordered when he tried pushing himself into a sitting position, the motion bringing a wave of pain and nausea.

"Lauren," he moaned, falling back to the leaf-littered ground. "I'll always love you," he whispered before darkness blanketed him in a comforting cocoon of painless respite.

He was still, too still. It was like it had been only months before, but this time Cal was not feigning an injury. His shallow breathing and the moisture bathing his face indicated he was going into shock, and this time Lauren didn't hesitate to leave him, racing to the house to call for emergency medical assistance.

She completed the call, grabbed a blanket from a closet, then returned to Cal. Scrap had also come back, settling down on his master's middle.

Lauren shooed the cat away and covered Cal with the blanket. She then sat down beside him and prayed.

"Your husband has suffered a concussion, Mrs. Samuels."

"No broken bones?" Lauren asked the tall, imposing physician.

"His x-rays are negative."

"When can I take him home?"

The doctor ran a hand through a shock of thick graying

hair. "We'd like to keep him in a quiet, darkened environment for at least two days. He's young and in excellent health, therefore I don't expect any complications."

Lauren nodded, chewing her lower lip. "May I see him?"

The doctor registered her apprehension. "Of course, Mrs. Samuels." He led her down a corridor and into Cal's room.

She stepped into the darkened room, barely making out the still form on the bed. She moved closer to the bed and reached for Cal's hand. He did not respond to the slight pressure of her fingers. Raising his limp hand, Lauren kissed his long, beautifully tapered fingers.

"I love you, Caleb Samuels," she murmured against his palm.

Cal heard the softly spoken words yet he could not bring himself to respond. The pain—dull, throbbing and relentless—detached his brain from his body.

"I'll be back later, sweetheart," she crooned in the low, soothing voice Cal treasured.

She released his hand and suddenly he felt cold; cold and alone with his private pain.

"When are you going to get some sleep, Lauren?" Odessa asked her daughter.

"Tonight. Cal's home and now I can relax."

Odessa stared at Lauren, noting the deep hollows in her cheeks and the circles under her large eyes. It appeared as if Lauren had taken her role as wife seriously: in sickness and in health.

"You love him, don't you?" Odessa questioned directly.

Lauren's head swung around and she returned her direct stare. At another time she would have denied the truth, but now she knew it was hopeless and useless to do so.

"Yes," she answered after a quiet moment. "I love Cal very, very much."

Odessa's face brightened with a beautiful smile. "Does this mean that you two don't plan to divorce or annul your marriage after a year?"

"Yes."

Odessa crossed her arms under her breasts, grinning. "When can I expect another grandchild?"

Lauren felt a ripple of excitement throughout her body. Cal's accident had disrupted her normal routine and she hadn't thought about taking her contraceptives. As it was, she had to call her doctor for an appointment before he wrote another prescription.

"As soon as I discuss it with your son-in-law," Lauren stated with a smile that matched Odessa's wide grin.

"Don't wait too long, Lauren."

"I won't, Mama." She had told her mother the truth— she wouldn't wait too long.

Cal had been home for more than a week yet he hadn't resumed writing. Most times he lay in bed hours after Lauren rose, gritting his teeth against the bright light inching through the drawn drapes.

He hadn't complained about the dull pain racking his head, but he knew he couldn't continue to hide it from Lauren.

Cal heard a soft meow and turned his head slowly. Scrap crept into the bedroom and stood by the bed. Lifting a hand, he motioned to the kitten.

Scrap sprang to the bed and settled himself at the foot, burrowing down into a comfortable position on the thick comforter. In the past Lauren had screamed about having animals in her house and, in particular, on her bed but lately nothing seemed to upset her.

Last night she had broached the subject of their having another child and if he hadn't been in so much pain they would have started immediately.

Cal wanted another child. The thought wrung a wry

smile from him; this time he and Lauren would have a glorious time making a baby.

"Mail call," came Lauren's throaty voice, breaking into his reverie.

Cal pushed himself up against a mound of pillows and extended his hand. He noted Lauren's slight scowl at the small mound of fur at the foot of the bed, but it vanished quickly.

She handed Cal a stack of envelopes and magazines, then floated down beside him. Scrap stirred, opened one gold-green eye, yawned, then settled back to sleep.

"You know I can't abide animals on my bed," she mumbled, adjusting the pillows for Cal.

"Me or the cat?" he teased, tossing the thick stack of mail on his lap.

Lauren kissed his ear. "Not you. I'm talking about your furry friend who has hired himself out as your foot warmer."

"Do you care to replace him?" He gave her a pained, lecherous grin.

"Don't rush it, tiger. You're still not one hundred percent. I see you grimace when you don't think I'm looking."

"What else do you see, all-knowing wife?"

"It's not what I see, Caleb, but what I know. And I know you're not up to a wrestling match." Leaning over, she kissed his forehead. "I'll be back later."

Cal's right hand captured her chin and he held her gently while pressing his lips to hers. "I'll join you for lunch."

Lauren smiled, running a forefinger down the length of his nose. "I thought you enjoyed having your meals in bed."

He released her. "I enjoy having only you in my bed."

"Me and Scrap." Lauren blew him a kiss and walked out of the bedroom.

Cal smiled and settled back against the pillows. Lauren

was right. Somehow he couldn't resist the friendly, cuddly little kitten. It followed him around and meowed to be held. Scrap had become more his pet than Drew's.

He stared down at the stack of envelopes on his lap, recognizing the return address of his agent. He had completed a detailed outline and the first five chapters of his new novel.

Opening the envelope, Cal scanned the one-page letter quickly. A wide smile creased his face. Three major publishers were interested in his work and the agent was scheduled to auction it the following month.

I still have it, he thought. The five-year drought of not writing or completing anything was over. He had not depleted his creative reservoir, and *Cross of Deception* would become a bestseller. He was certain of that, and only now would he show Lauren what he had written. They would celebrate together.

Cal slipped a letter opener under the flap of a kraft envelope, shaking out its contents. As the glossy photos spilled out on the comforter, the breath was sucked from his lungs. The pain in his temples intensified as he gritted his teeth and groaned audibly.

"No!" His intense pain bounced off the bedroom walls as he flung the envelope and its contents off the bed.

All of his joy vanished with the images on the slick paper. Pain he thought he would never feel again slashed at him relentlessly, coming in waves.

"Not again," he hissed through clenched teeth. "Not again!"

Lauren retreated to her study and opened her own mail. Opening envelopes, she stacked pamphlets and sheaths of pages in differing piles. She had received the information she sought on the beginning and spread of Islam throughout northern Africa. It was what she needed to complete her research for Cal.

She opened a kraft envelope similar to the one Cal had received. The photos slid out and she felt the floor come up at her.

How could she explain? The photos were too real, too damaging to refute. The image of her in Andrew's arms, eyes closed, her head against his chest and his chin resting on her head said it all. She looked like a sated woman in the arms of her lover.

Someone had taken a photograph of her and Andrew when they shared the dance at Off the Beaten Path the weekend Cal had gone fishing with Drew.

Jacqueline Samuels!

It had to be her or she had put someone up to do it.

The phone rang and Lauren snatched up the receiver. "Hello." Her voice was breathless, as if she had run a grueling race.

"Did you see this morning's *Globe*?" came Gwen Taylor's hushed voice.

Lauren bit down hard on her lower lip to stop its trembling. "I think I know what's in it."

"Oh, cuz, I'm so sorry. Usually I'd get wind that something like this is going to blow. But this time it was very hush-hush." There was a pause before Gwen said, "Does Caleb know?"

"I don't know," Lauren replied, still stunned, "but I'm certain he'll find out soon enough. Which means I'm going to have to explain everything before it blows up into something neither of us will be able to control."

"Good luck, cuz. After I hang up I'm going to find out who took those pictures and sent them in. There's one sex biscuit at the *Globe* who has been after me for more than a year to go out with him. I think I'll call him up and interrogate the sweet, sticky honey bun. Bye!"

Lauren replaced the receiver, gathering the damaging photographs. With a heavy heart and a heavy step she walked out of her study and down the stairs.

Yes, he knows, she thought, the moment she saw the

photographs strewn over the bedroom carpet. The glossy black and white photos in Lauren's hands fluttered to the floor when she saw Cal hold his arms out to her.

Relief girded her limbs as she raced across the room and flung herself against her husband. His warmth, his strength and his love flowed through her.

"Caleb, Caleb," she whispered over and over, as much from relief as from shame. "I only danced with him."

Cal captured her chin between his thumb and forefinger, raising her face. He surveyed her trembling mouth and the profound pain in her midnight eyes.

"I know that and you know that," he stated with a smile.

"But—but it's in this morning's *Globe*. Gwen just called and told me."

Cal ran a hand through the thick curls of her hair. "It's all right." He nodded when her eyes widened.

"But don't you care, Caleb?"

"Of course I care, darling." There was a lethal calmness in his eyes. "And I'm going to find out who took those pictures and who sent them to the *Globe*." He didn't tell her that he suspected Jacqueline.

The phone rang, preempting what Lauren had to tell Cal. He picked it up after the first ring. "Hello."

"This is Andrew. May I speak to Lauren?"

"I think it's better that you speak to me, Monroe. Lauren's rather upset right now."

"I'm more than upset," Andrew shouted. "Right now I'm about as mean as cat piss."

Cal stared at the cat at the foot of his bed. He didn't think Scrap would appreciate Andrew's reference to cats.

"I think we should discuss this without losing our heads," Cal suggested.

"I'm on my way," came Andrew's reply.

Lauren watched Cal hang up the telephone, his features settling into a stern loathing.

"Jacqueline was at Off the Beaten Path the night I was there," she informed Cal.

His expression did not change. "But she didn't take the photos. They were taken by a professional. This is not the first time she has done something like this and I want to catch both Jacqueline and her flunky in the same trap."

Lauren frowned. "What are you talking about?"

"Jacqueline sent my father damaging photographs of her kissing me."

"But how did you come to kiss her if you didn't date her?"

"She had someone take the picture when I congratulated her after she'd been signed to a record deal. It was the only time I'd ever kissed her, because even though I never liked my father's wife I was happy for her at that moment. Of course it caused a rift between me and my father that never healed. He died of a massive heart attack a month later."

Lauren digested this, unable to believe that someone would go through such lengths to destroy lives. "What are you going to do?"

"Beat Jacqueline Samuels at her own game."

"That's telling me exactly nothing, Caleb Samuels." Lauren felt her own temper rise.

He threw off the sheet and blanket. "Excuse me, Lauren, but I must get dressed." He headed for the bathroom, leaving her staring at his magnificent naked male body.

Lauren sank down to the bed and lay staring up at the ceiling. She refused to think about what was to come. But she knew Jacqueline had to be stopped. Stopped before she harmed Drew.

Right now Drew was too young to read headline captions in tabloid gossip columns, but he wasn't too young not to understand virulent gossip repeated by adults and older children.

Closing her eyes, Lauren waited for her husband.

Chapter Fifteen

Lauren, Cal and Andrew sat at the kitchen table, analyzing Jacqueline Samuels.

"Do you think she'll try something like this again?" Andrew questioned.

"Not if we don't give her an opportunity," Lauren replied. "My meeting you at the club and dancing with you was a stroke of luck for Jacqueline." She glanced over at a frowning Cal. "It will not happen again."

"That may be true, however I don't intend to spend my life looking over my shoulder, hoping someone isn't lurking in the background with a camera ready to take incriminating pictures of my family," Cal stated, his frown deepening. He slid off the bench. "Excuse me. I have to take something for this headache."

Lauren stood with him, placing a hand on his arm. "How bad is it?"

He tried smiling but it was more a grimace than a smile. "Not too bad," he lied. Lauren dropped her hand and he walked out of the kitchen.

He's lying, she thought. Touching his arm revealed a rigidness associated with intense pain and/or tension. It was enough that Cal had to deal with recovering from a concussion, but having to deal with Jacqueline Samuels's treachery was another matter.

It was then that Lauren decided to take control of her

life and her marriage. "I'd like you to leave, Andrew. Cal's tired and in pain. Dealing with Jacqueline will have to wait."

"But he wanted . . ."

"He can't, Andrew," she interrupted.

Andrew rose to his feet and stared down at Lauren, complete surprise on his face. "Are you certain this is what you want?"

"It is," she replied in a firm tone.

"Jacqueline Samuels can't hurt me, Lauren," Andrew insisted. "It's you and Caleb she wants . . ."

"We'll discuss this some other time," Lauren cut in. Rising on tiptoe, she kissed his smooth cheek. "Thank you for coming."

Andrew shrugged his shoulders, nodding. "Let me know when you and Caleb are ready to tar and feather our nemesis."

Lauren saw Andrew to the door and watched him drive away. What Andrew did not know was that Jacqueline did not want to hurt her or Cal. She wanted Drew's money; money she felt belonged to her; money Dr. Caleb Samuels denied her; money she needed. But for what?

Cal had disclosed that his father provided generously for Jacqueline in his will. She had been left with property, bonds and cash, and David Samuels had not been dead that long for Jacqueline to have exhausted her resources—or had she?

"Where's Monroe?"

Lauren turned at the sound of Cal's voice and she gave him a warm smile. "He had to leave."

Cal massaged his temples with his forefingers. "It's just as well. I've had enough of Jacqueline for one day."

She moved to his side and wound an arm around his waist. "What do you say we go for a walk, eat lunch out, then come back here and relax before Drew gets home from school?"

Cal cradled her head to his shoulder. "That sounds like a wonderful idea."

Lauren flashed a tender, open smile. "I'll be right back. I need a jacket."

"I'll wait on the porch for you," he replied, opening the front door.

He stepped out onto the porch, inhaling the crisp autumn air. The trees were a riot of color: yellow, orange, red and varying shades of gold against towering evergreens.

Cal felt the band of tightness around his forehead easing. The medication was working quickly, and for the first time in a week he was pain-free.

He was pain-free and gloriously happy, and he had Lauren and his grandfather to thank for that.

Lauren was perfect—perfect in every way—in or out of bed.

No one, and that included Jacqueline, could do anything that would disrupt his marriage to Lauren.

The storm door slammed and Cal turned, finding Lauren dressed in a pair of jeans, sweater, lightweight jacket and a pair of wool gloves. So much for a jacket.

He threw back his head and laughed, the sound floating upward and startling several birds perched on trees near the house. They screeched, flew several feet, then settled back to warming themselves in the bright fall sun.

Cal held Lauren's hands firmly between his own. "I don't think you're going to need these, precious. It's not freezing."

"It's forty-two degrees and that's cold enough for me."

"I'll keep you warm," he crooned, pulling the gloves from her hands and slipping them into the pockets of his beige cords. He pulled her right hand into the curve of his arm over a thick cotton sweater.

"What about this one?" She held up a small, well-groomed hand.

"Put it in your jacket pocket."

Lauren shifted, pushing her hand up under his sweater. Her fingers caressed bare skin. "I prefer this kind of warmth, Caleb Samuels," she sighed, resting her head on his chest.

His insides melted in sensual excitement. The feel of Lauren's fingertips floating over his breasts was unbearable and his body reacted violently.

Without warning, she was lifted into the cradle of his arms. "I think the walk is out this morning," he stated hoarsely, his warm breath fanning Lauren's upturned face.

She lowered her gaze in a demure gesture. "What do you want to do instead?"

Cal turned back to the front door. "Let's see if we can't go about increasing our family. I never liked being an only child."

"Neither did I," she replied, burying her face against his hard shoulder.

Cal opened the door, stepped inside the house, then kicked it closed with his foot. "Boy or girl?"

"It doesn't matter," Lauren murmured, closing her eyes as Cal carried her across the living room and up the staircase to the second floor. "As long as it is healthy."

"I'm partial to a girl," he replied, walking into the bedroom and lowering Lauren on the bed. "A little girl who looks exactly like her mother."

"I'm willing to bet it will probably look exactly like . . ."

Her words were stopped when Cal's mouth covered hers possessively.

Everything stopped and was forgotten—even Jacqueline Samuels's attempt to destroy their marriage—when Lauren and Cal abandoned themselves to the fires engulfing them with the erotic passion that had eluded them for weeks.

* * *

Two days later Gwen's source came through with the information Lauren and Cal needed to unravel Jacqueline's plot to secure Drew's money.

Jacqueline had paid the photographer with a check drawn on her recording company's account, but it had bounced. The photgrapher was more than willing to disclose that Jacqueline had not made good on the check.

"So you see, cuz, it appears as if the lady has money problems. What I don't understand is why. It's been rumored that her company is raking in the dough."

Gwen leaned closer to be heard over the incessant babble of voices at the Harvard Book Store Café. Lunch at the popular dining establishment was always like a family reunion. You never knew who you would meet and everyone appeared to talk at once.

"Maybe Jacqueline's company needs an audit," Lauren mused aloud.

"I know a sex muffin at the IRS who just might like to look into a certain record company's books, if you know what I mean," Gwen suggested.

If the situation hadn't been so serious Lauren would've laughed. Gwen Taylor knew more sex muffins and biscuits at more places than she had fingers and toes.

Lauren opened her mouth, but Gwen held up her hand. "Say no more, cousin. Consider this a done deal."

"How can I thank you, Gwen?"

Gwen leaned over and hugged her cousin. "Get me an interview with Caleb Samuels."

Lauren hugged her back. "Done."

Gwen's smile faltered. "Are you certain he'll agree to it? You know he's never agreed to be interviewed. That's why there's always been so much made-up gossip about him."

"I'll get him to change his mind," Lauren promised.

"It's like *that?*" Gwen retorted, shifting her eyebrows.

"Yes, it is, cuz," Lauren said smugly.

"Well, girl, I must say you really have it going on if you can accomplish this feat." Gwen glanced down at her watch and gasped. "If I don't hurry I'm going to be late for a departmental meeting."

"I'll drop you off," Lauren offered.

"Thanks." Gwen gathered her handbag and leather-bound notebook.

Lauren drove Gwen back to the *Boston Gazette* building, thanking her again for all of her help. Gwen shrugged it off with a wave and a smile.

"Don't worry, cuz. It's just about over."

The four words echoed in Lauren's head as she turned her car in the direction of North Grafton. It had to be over so that she and Cal could live their lives without the invisible fears threatening to drive them apart, and she prayed it would be soon.

"Lauren! Lauren! Darling, look at the headlines!"

Lauren scrambled from the bed, not bothering to put on a robe or slippers. She met Cal as he bounded up the staircase.

He eased her down to the top step and sat beside her. Flicking open the *Boston Herald* he showed her the blaring headline: RECORDING EXEC INDICTED IN PIRATE SCAM.

It was enough. Lauren did not have to read further. The photograph of Jacqueline Harvell Samuels, handcuffed and head lowered was victory enough.

She stared at the photo of the defeated woman. "I feel sorry for her, Cal."

Cal raised her chin. "Don't, baby. Jacqueline brought all of this on herself. She just rolled the dice once too often and they came up craps."

He gathered Lauren in his arms, stood up and made his

way back to the bedroom. She nuzzled her nose to his warm throat, inhaling the smell of the early morning air still lingering on his skin.

Cal dropped the newspaper on the floor by the door, then settled Lauren on the bed. Stripping off his robe, he melted into her outstretched arms, naked and wanting.

"Now, we're truly free," Lauren breathed into his mouth.

Cal moaned and entered her willing body. Yes, they were free; just like the characters in his book, they had shattered their bonds to find the freedom to live and love for future generations of proud African descendants.

Epilogue

"Mr. Samuels, can you hold your daughter so that we can get a family shot?"

Cal reached for the squirming eleven-month-old child. Kayla had just learned to walk and she did not like sitting still for more than thirty seconds.

"Drew, please stand next to your mother," the photographer directed softly.

Drew leaned against Lauren's shoulder as she sat on the wicker love seat.

Cal managed to catch and hold onto Kayla, although the child protested loudly against his firm hold on her body.

He tossed her high in the air, then whispered in her ear. The petite, golden-eyed girl giggled uncontrollably.

"Let's do it now," Cal called to the photographer as he sat down beside Lauren.

The photographer got off three frames before Kayla's giggles vanished. "Wonderful. Thank you very much."

Drew fidgeted with his white bow tie. "Can I change now?"

"Yes," Lauren and Cal replied in unison.

"Da-da, Da-da," Kayla repeated in a rhythmic sing-song, patting Cal's face with her tiny hands.

He kissed her forehead. "You want to change, too?" They all moved inside the house.

"Ma-ma, Ma-ma," Kayla cried, holding her arms out to her mother.

Lauren took her daughter from Cal, smiling. "I know what kind of changing she needs."

"She never wants me to change her," Cal said, taking off his jacket and tie.

"That's because you don't sing to her," Lauren said over her shoulder as she started up the staircase.

Cal stood at the foot of the staircase, watching Lauren ascend slowly with their daughter cradled gently in her arms.

Their home was filled with family and friends—well-wishers who had come to help him celebrate the success of his latest book. It had made it to first place on all of the major bestseller lists.

Cal had dedicated this book to Lauren and their own captive hearts, knowing when he sat down to write it that she had already captured his heart many years before on a private island in the Caribbean.

"Caleb."

He glanced up at Lauren standing at the top of the staircase. "Yes?"

She offered him a shy smile. "The next one is going to look like me."

She walked away, leaving him with his mouth gaping in shock. He sank down to a step, laughing. Lauren always thought of the most unorthodox ways of telling him that he was going to be a father.

He was still laughing when Roy Taylor came to tell him that everyone was waiting for him to say a few words.

Cal stood up, whispered the latest news in Roy's ear and the two men shook hands and pounded each other's backs.

"I must say that you turn out some beautiful children," Roy complimented.

Cal patted his father-in-law's back again. "Why thank you, Roy."

"Don't give him all of the credit, Daddy. He couldn't do it without my help."

Both men turned at the sound of the throaty feminine voice. They were not aware that she had silently come down the stairs.

"And don't you ever forget that, *precious,*" she added, flashing Cal a sensual smile.

"I won't, *precious,*" he replied, taking Kayla from her mother's arms and setting her on her feet.

Lauren and Cal lingered before going out to the patio to join their guests.

"Did I show you how much I loved you today?" Cal crooned against her ear.

"I don't think so," Lauren answered gently. "But I'm not opposed to a demonstration. Later, that is."

"Then later it will be."

Lauren and Cal had many more times and many more years to prove their love to each other—again and again, over and over.